W9-DGF-956

Miss Frost
solves a Cold Case

A Nocturne Falls Mystery
Jayne Frost, book one

KRISTEN PAINTER

MISS FROST SOLVES A COLD CASE
A Nocturne Falls Mystery
Jayne Frost, Book One

Copyright © 2016 Kristen Painter

All rights reserved. No part of this book may be reproduced in any form or by any electronic or mechanical means, including information storage and retrieval systems—except in the case of brief quotations embodied in critical articles or reviews—without permission in writing from the author.

This book is a work of fiction. The characters, events, and places portrayed in this book are products of the author's imagination and are either fictitious or are used fictitiously. Any similarity to real person, living or dead, is purely coincidental and not intended by the author.

ISBN: 978-1-941695-17-3

Published in the United States of America.

Welcome to Nocturne Falls — the town that celebrates Halloween 365 days a year.

Jayne Frost is a lot of things. Winter elf, Jack Frost's daughter, Santa Claus's niece, heir to the Winter Throne and now…private investigator. Sort of.

Needing someone he can trust, her father sends her undercover to Nocturne Falls to find out why employees at the Santa's Workshop toy store are going missing.

Doing that requires getting to know the town, which leads to interesting encounters with a sexy vampire, an old flame, and an elevator that's strictly off-limits. The more Jayne finds out, the more questions she has, but the answers lead her deeper into danger.

Will her magic save her? Or will she come up cold?

I knew the minute I walked into my father's office, this wasn't going to be one of those friendly father-daughter, how's-life-treating-you conversations.

Not a chance. Right now the man I was looking at wasn't so much my father as he was the Winter King, and I was more one of his subjects than his darling daughter. It happened. I understood. I suppose I wasn't always the easiest elf to be around. Although, in my own defense, I really don't dwell on the fact that I'm a princess.

And hey, he had a job to do (we all did), but in his case, despite being the Winter King, he still had to report to the fat man in the red suit. Not that any of us called Uncle Kris that to his face.

Some days, I really felt for my dad. Being the Winter King and Santa's right-hand man wasn't an easy job. And other days, I reminded myself that he had to have known what he was getting into. I mean, you don't marry Klara Kringle, join the family business and think your life's going to stay the same.

Even if you are royalty in the elf world.

But I digress.

"Hi, Dad." Never a bad idea to remind him of our familial relationship.

"Jayne. Have a seat."

Jayne, not Jay. This was serious business. I took a chair across from the slab of glacier he called a desk.

He sighed, letting out an icy cloud of vapor. More because of who he was than the temperature in the room, but this was the North Pole, and we were winter elves. Cold was our jam. He looked at me. "We have an issue."

I bristled a little, going on the defensive. "Whatever the second shift said, I did not know those cartons were full of breakables."

He frowned. "I'm not talking about that."

"Oh." I relaxed. "Then…what's up? Let me guess, I'm getting moved to a different department again."

He shoved a hand through his dark blue hair, causing it to spike up even higher. "You've had some trouble finding your place here, that's true, but it's important you understand every aspect of the company."

At least he left out how I was almost thirty. I crossed my arms and slouched a little. "Do you know what it's like being your daughter and working here?"

He nodded. "I understand there are some difficulties related to who you are."

"*Some* difficulties? People either ignore me entirely or are so phony nice to me that my teeth ache from the sickening sweetness of it all."

"What about Lark?"

"Dad, Lark went to Europe to find herself and ended up becoming a world-famous DJ." I missed my BFF, but she'd been gone for almost ten years now. I'd resigned myself to the fact that my only real friend had a new life. Since she'd left, she'd only been back three times. But I understood. She was seeing the world and living like a rock star (or so I imagined), and I was double-checking how many times little Johnny Human had sassed his mother. The North Pole just wasn't her home anymore.

His brows scrunched together into a dark blue vee. "You could have done something else after college."

I barked out a laugh. "You're the one who asked me to come back here after graduation. I could have totally gone into communications like I'd planned, but no, you said, 'Jayne, come home, join the family business, get to know how things work, then you can take over for me one day and—'"

He held up his hand. "I did ask. You're right. And you still will take over for me one day. It's inevitable. You're my only child."

I snorted. I had cousins. I wasn't *really* the only option. I was just closest in line. "I love that I get the job regardless of how qualified I am for it."

He gave me a very fatherly look. "I do want you to be happy."

"I am happy." Mostly. But didn't everyone get that feeling like there was something else to discover? Something they were, I don't know, missing out on? "Being close to you and Mom is great. There's no substitute for family, right?"

"Right." He sighed, sending another cloud of vapor into the air. "That's part of why I'm giving you a new assignment."

I sat up. "A new assignment? You didn't say *job*, so I'm thinking this isn't just a change from monitoring the Naughty & Nice list to manager of the employee cafeteria. Although, I could definitely do that." Not that working the N & N list wasn't a cushy gig. It was. But everyone knew I'd been put there to keep my interactions with the other employees to a minimum. And managing the cafeteria would mean direct access to the desserts. Which were pretty major. Elves like sweets. A lot.

"It's not. It's more than that. Far more." He pulled out a file and opened it. Yes, we still use a lot of paper in the NP. Electronics go a little nuts up here. We still use them, but there's never a guarantee you'll get a signal. "You know we maintain a chain of toy stores around the world for testing new products and staying in touch with our demographic."

"Yep. Santa's Workshop." Everyone knew about the toy stores. Getting sent to work at one of them was sort of like being sent to prison, but with worse food. Okay, maybe it wasn't that bad, but you had to deal with humans, there was zero chance for advancement, and you had to deal with humans. And their children. Lots and lots of their children.

I'm not always such a people person. Did I mention that?

Anyway, apparently some elves actually *wanted* to work in the stores, because there was a waiting list and an interview process and blah, blah, blah. Whatever. Those elves were weird.

"The flagship store in Nocturne Falls has been having some attrition issues."

"In English, please."

"Workers are quitting without notice. Well, they're leaving a note, but that's it. Basically they're just not showing up for their shifts. It's been going on for nearly three years, but not in a noticeable way."

"Then how did it get noticed?"

"The Elf Census. One of our statisticians noticed

5

that six of our citizens weren't accounted for, and those six were last listed as employed at the Santa's Workshop in Nocturne Falls."

"So they didn't come back to the NP. It happens." Lark was a prime example of that. "It's not required, is it?"

"No. Most do though. And to have no record of these six when they all worked at the same store and quit unexpectedly? It's just odd."

"I agree. So what do you think is happening?"

"We don't know. Could be they're being lured away by the appeal of the human world or a competing business, or we're having some other issue at that particular store, or something else going on in that town, but we have to figure it out. That's a busy store, and we can't afford to be constantly understaffed or have these kinds of problems."

I hated to see my dad upset. "Who's the manager?"

"Tolliver Featherstone. Took the job as his retirement about three years ago."

"Which is as long as the elves have been leaving. But I can't imagine they're leaving because of him." He'd been the head tinker for ages and had invented more best-selling toys than any other before him. The saying went, if Toly touched it, it was gold. "Featherstone is kind of a legend."

My father nodded. "That's how he got the job at

6

the store. He was infinitely qualified, so when he asked, it was a done deal. He's got a granddaughter who lives in town. He wanted to be close to her but keep his hand in the business. We don't think it has anything to do with him either, but we don't really know at this point."

"Was the previous manager reassigned to make room for him?"

"No. She retired for good. A month later, Toly took over."

I squinted at him. "Where do I come into all this?"

He put a slim, silver bracelet on the desk and slid it toward me. I knew exactly what it was. Lots of us used them to hide our elfiness from humans when we left the NP. "You're going undercover as the newest employee. This bracelet isn't like the usual ones. It won't mask that you're an elf, but it will hide your true identity as long as you have it on, transforming you into a normal winter elf. Not Jayne Frost, Winter Princess."

"What about on the way to Nocturne Falls?"

"Just wear your regular bracelet. The two magics are compatible. It won't lessen your abilities, though, so when you get to the store, you'll have to watch how much magic you use in front of the other employees."

Because my skill level would give me away as being more than just a normal winter elf. "Got it."

"Then you're all set."

Notice he didn't ask if I'd like to go, just told me what I was going to be doing like that was that. Which, I guess it was. When Jack Frost gave you an order, you pretty much did as you were told. "You said the bracelet won't hide that I'm an elf. Should I keep my other bracelet on then? Won't my ears and my blue hair be an issue when I'm in town?" Assuming my new identity still had blue hair.

"Not in Nocturne Falls. Supernaturals live as themselves without issue. It's how the town is set up. You'll see."

A town where I could be exactly who I was? That was interesting. "And I'm the one best for this because?"

"Because you're family and we trust you. And we need someone we trust in this situation."

"We meaning you and Uncle Kris?"

"Yes. And your mother and your aunt Martha, of course."

"Good to know it's not just a ploy to get rid of me."

He laughed. "No, sweetheart. It really is about getting someone we trust in on the ground floor. You know how seriously Kris takes those stores. If there's a problem, he wants it solved."

That was flattering. At least I knew they trusted me, even if I didn't always make them happy. I reached for the bracelet. It gleamed blue in the light, a sure sign of elf magic. "And if—I mean, *when* I get to the bottom of this?"

"Then we'll bring you home and figure out something else for you to do. Something you like more."

"I don't hate working the N & N list, but something in design might be cool." Kind of sad that I still felt adrift in my own community at this age. But then princess was a title, not a job. At least not one that was full time. I tucked the bracelet in my pocket. "When do I leave?"

"Tonight. Toly knows a new worker is scheduled to arrive in a couple days. We own the whole building there, as we do with all our stores, so one of the upper-floor apartments will be yours for as long as you need."

I laughed. "You were pretty sure I was going to say yes, huh? Not that you actually asked..."

He skimmed over that. "There's one more thing. You know magic is really the only way we can communicate from the North Pole, so we've come up with something." He placed two identical snow globes on his desk. Both of them were empty except for the snow, and each had a pretty snowflake design on the front.

"Magical cell phones were out of the question?"

He ignored my snarky comment, picking up one of the snow globes instead. "Watch the other globe." He gave the one in his hand a good shake, and a few seconds later, the snow in the second globe began swirling. "When you see the snow falling, pick up your globe and push the button on the back."

I reached over and took the second globe. Sure enough, there was a small button recessed into the back. I pushed it. "Now what?"

My image showed up in the globe in my dad's hand and my voice echoed back at me.

He grinned. "Now we can communicate."

His image and voice came through mine. "Wow. That's cool. About time the NP got its own version of Skype."

He pushed the button on his, and the snow stopped swirling. "Keep it near you at all times when you're in your apartment."

"Will do." Although, probably not too near. I mean, how much could he see through that thing?

"Good." Then he handed me the thick file on his desk. "This has everything in it that you need to know. Memorize it on the flight down. There's also a credit card in there with your alias on it. Use it for whatever you need."

I took the file. "Speaking of the flight, please tell me it's first class."

"Not this time. From this moment on, you're not the princess anymore." He let out a soft sigh and folded his hands on the desktop. "Jay, be careful down there. Like I said, Nocturne Falls isn't like most human towns. It's…different. Alluring."

"You think I'm going to fall in love with the place and want to stay? Don't worry about that. I'm a winter elf. I live at the North Pole." I gave him a smile. "Nothing's going to change that."

Nocturne Falls was crazy. Cray-zee.

Halloween twenty-four seven, three hundred and sixty five. Sure, there were towns that did the year-round Christmas thing, but when you live at the North Pole and work in Santa's factory, that doesn't seem unusual at all.

This place, on the other hand, was wild. The whole town was themed in full-on Halloween. From the black, orange, purple, and green color scheme to the crooked buildings to the spooky street names to the permanently cobwebbed lamp posts, Nocturne Falls made no bones about what happened here. I was a little in love already. There were even old-school Halloween characters walking around taking pictures with people. I passed a witch before I'd been on the street for ten minutes.

But let me back up, because I'd been here longer

than that. I'd landed, found the ride my father had arranged from the airport, and made it into town an hour ago. But my first stop was a diner called Mummy's where I scarfed down two surprisingly good slices of pie (one chocolate silk, one banana cream) and washed them down with a vanilla milkshake. A really good vanilla milkshake.

I know by human standards that's not exactly a balanced breakfast. Or lunch. Or whatever meal I was supposed to be eating at this time of day, but I think I mentioned elves like sweets. A lot. Fortunately, we have the typical high-powered supernatural metabolism to go along with the ramped-up sweet tooth.

And with all the traveling and time changes, I needed sugar to make me right again. The pie and milkshake had done the job.

Now I was dragging two rolling suitcases down Main Street, looking for the shop so I could check in with Toly and get the key to my apartment. I would have used the nav on my phone, but it's kind of hard to hold a phone, drag two suitcases, and shoulder a laptop case on one side and a purse on the other while trying to avoid accidentally cold-cocking tourists all at the same time.

A few streets in and my eyes started to glaze over from all the orange and black and purple and black and green and, well, you get the idea. Then a bright red and green sign trimmed in gold popped into my field of vision like a Christmas miracle.

Santa's Workshop. At last.

The faded red brick building was three stories, with the shop taking up the first floor and apartments for employees occupying the upper two. It wasn't mandatory that workers lived in the company housing, but it was a perk of the job, and who was going to turn down a free place to live? The apartments probably weren't the Four Seasons or anything (which is where we stayed when we went to New York City), but I was sure they weren't dumps either.

I'd know soon enough.

As mentioned, most of the stores in Nocturne Falls adhered pretty heavily to the Halloween theme, but Santa's Workshop was one hundred percent Christmas. Right down to the *genuine* icicles hanging off the eaves and the canopy over the door, and the swirls of frost in the corners of the windows. When the sun caught the building just right, the glow of blue was noticeable. At least to my eyes.

Because making real ice and frost happen in Georgia in April? That was winter elf magic right there, but not all winter elves could maintain that level of magic over a sustained period of time. I could, but I was Jack Frost's daughter. My skills were above average.

This had to be Toly's work. And based on the

amount of selfies being taken next to the biggest clump of icicles, I'd say those real icicles were quite the tourist attraction. I'm sure they thought there was some kind of chiller system built into the place.

I got closer and waited for a kind soul to hold the door, then dragged myself and my worldly possessions inside.

The spacious store smelled of pine, snow (yes, that's a smell), and peppermint. The combination reminded me of home. The shelves were packed with toys. A big room in the back provided a place for kids to play with any toy in the store they wanted to. Twinkling fairy lights covered the ceiling, bins on the floor held more toys, and magic seemed to glitter in the air.

Maybe that was just something elves could see, but the looks on the customers' faces could only be described as enchanted. The place was pretty amazing.

And despite the crush of tourists wandering through the store, Toly wasn't hard to pick out.

Winter elves are as diverse as any other kind of supernatural. We're tall, short, thin, fat (despite the metabolism, it does happen to some of us as we get older), light-skinned, dark-skinned, even blue-skinned on occasion. Our hair and eye colors have the same variations as humans, although, our hair can also run in shades from silvery white to deepest blue, but those colors tend to signify greater magical powers.

In general, we tend to be a fairly elegant bunch. More *Lord of the Rings* than cookie-bakers in trees, if you get my drift.

Toly, however, was pushing cookie-baker pretty hard. Most tinkers seemed to go that way. He was short and plump, with tufts of white hair that ringed his head leaving a shiny bald spot on top. The half-moon glasses perched on the end of his round nose did nothing to hide his twinkling eyes. He was talking to a little boy near the toy trains, and he hadn't stopped smiling since I'd spotted him.

His rosy cheeks were probably always that color.

In short, Toly was the winter elf equivalent of a Hallmark grandpa. He handed the little boy a train, patted him on the head and looked up.

His eyes met mine, and his jolly smile somehow got bigger. He headed toward me, hand out. "You must be our new salesperson."

I dropped the handle of one suitcase to shake his hand. It was warm and firm and comforting. "That's me."

"Well, hello there. And welcome to Santa's Workshop. I'm Tolliver Featherstone, but you probably already know that."

"Everybody knows who you are. I'm..." I remembered the dossier I'd studied on the way down. With my magic bracelet firmly in place, I wasn't Jayne Frost anymore. "Lilibeth Holiday."

Lilibeth was my middle name and Holiday was the most common last name among winter elves. Like Smith for humans. My dad had done well coming up with an identity that would be easy for me to remember and difficult for anyone else to deduce as false.

I guess being the Winter King also made him pretty sharp.

Toly put his gnarled hands on his wide hips. "Hi there, Lilibeth. Good to have you. I must say, you're a day earlier than I expected you, but that's fine, that's fine. I'm sure you'll want to get up to your apartment, then probably take a rest. It's a long trip."

"Yes, it was." Eighteen hours to be exact. And *not* in first class. At least I'd slept on the flight from Anchorage to Denver. After that, I'd gone into study mode, learning my new identity and those of the workers who'd quit.

Six workers over the last two and a half years was no big deal, except that the last two had left this year, and this year was only four months old.

Toly nodded, his expression going from jovial to concerned. "Well, we're glad you're here, but we don't want you worn out. And I imagine you'll want to see the town."

I did, and not just because it was part of my directive, but getting to meet my fellow employees seemed more important. "Don't you need me to get started right away?"

"Oh no, not today, dear. Tomorrow is soon enough. Better you're rested anyway."

"Well, I'll be good to go in the morning. I'm sure of it."

He nodded again. "Mm-hmm, mm-hmm, very good. Let's get you to your new apartment then. Right this way."

He didn't offer to take my bags, which was fine with me considering they were almost as tall as he was. He led me to a door marked Employees Only and pushed through it, holding it open until I and all my stuff passed by.

The space I walked into was drastically different from the shop. Cavernous and filled with row after row of metal shelving and two small, sectioned-off rooms, the area lived up to the Employees Only sign. This clearly wasn't a space for customers.

He waved a hand. "Welcome to the warehouse. It holds our Santa's Bag, the employee breakroom, and my office, but you can see all that tomorrow."

"Thanks." I wasn't sure what else there was to see, but I'd find out in the morning.

He pointed to a rack of three forest-green bikes parked against the far wall. "Those bikes are for employee use. So are the umbrellas in the stand there."

They were the same bikes we used in the NP to

travel through the Factory. In a place that big, you needed an efficient way to get around. "Corporate thinks of everything."

"Yes, they do, yes, they do." He shifted like he was trying to make himself taller. "When you come and go from your apartment and you're not working, that vestibule will take you outside without having to go through the shop. Your key works in that door as well." He pointed to a large door with a glass window that took up about half of it. It opened into a small lobby with another door, this one solid and heavy-looking with a small, wavy glass transom. "That leads out to a side street."

"Okay." There was an elevator in front of us, but through the vestibule door I could see another one. "Is that the elevator to the apartments or is it this one?"

His brows shot up, and his face took on a worried expression. "Oh, the elevator in the vestibule is not for us. We leave that be at all times. That's only for Nocturne Falls employees. This one in the warehouse takes us up to the apartments."

He leaned in and pushed the up button, his stubby finger covering the entire thing. "Won't be but a second."

I nodded, hoping he'd understand I was clear on leaving the other elevator alone. "Aren't we all kind of Nocturne Falls employees?"

He made a face as the elevator chimed and the doors slid open. "Oh no, dear. Technically, we're third-party vendors. Most of the real estate in this town is owned by the family who revived it. The Ellinghams. A nice enough bunch, considering."

I waited for a second, but he didn't elaborate. "Considering what?"

He waddled onto the lift, holding the doors until I got all my stuff on. Once I was in, he took his hand away and the doors slid shut. Then he answered my question, and when he did, his voice was low and conspiratorial. "They're *vampires*."

"Are you snowing me? That's cool." It honestly was. The North Pole is all elves all the time. Meeting some other kinds of supernaturals would be a lot of fun.

He frowned. "No, I'm not snowing you. They're really vampires. Old ones. Very powerful." He leaned in again, this time with a slight edge to his voice. "There are all kinds of creatures in this town. You have to be careful. Some of them are dangerous."

"Good to know. Thank you for sharing that with me." I wasn't worried. I could put a solid-as-steel icicle through a target at fifty paces. But could that be what was happening to the shop's workers? Were they being done in by some rogue supernatural who was killing them off then forging goodbye notes to make it seem like they'd simply left town? It was as plausible as any other explanation. It sure gave me another angle to consider.

And another reason to get to know more about the town and its citizens.

I kept up the conversation with Toly in hopes of getting a better read on him. "What happened to the employee I'm replacing? Did they get a promotion?"

Toly's brows lifted a moment, then scrunched back down. "No, no. The man quit."

"That's odd. Getting employed at Santa's Workshop is a pretty big deal."

Toly just nodded and mumbled something I didn't catch, and the elevator doors opened again, putting an end to that discussion as he announced we'd arrived.

We got out on the second floor. I followed him to the last door on the left. He dug into his apron pocket and pulled out a ring with two keys on it. "Your apartment is right here. 2D. This floor has four apartments, and the upstairs has three. Those apartments are a little bigger, but the largest is reserved for visitors from corporate."

Like my father or my uncle. I took the key ring Toly offered. "Does corporate send people frequently?"

He shrugged. "Once in a while. Same as most stores, I'd imagine."

"Okay." I wasn't sure what else to say to that. "I guess I'll get settled in. Which key is for the apartment?"

"The brass one. The silver one is for the store and the warehouse door. That key contains a little magic that acts as an identifying chip. It eliminates the need for our employees to have a keycard or anything extra. Wi-Fi is SantaNet, password is Reindeer, but if you forget, it's written on the back of the TV remote."

I could see a blue shine on the silver key when I tilted it. More elf magic. "Perfect."

He smiled. "Housekeeping comes once a week, which is tomorrow. They take care of linens too."

"Nice." I hadn't counted on that. Not that I'd necessarily be here that long. "Makes life easier, huh?"

"It does, it does. We're well taken care of."

So why were employees leaving?

He smoothed his apron. "I'll let you be then. We open at ten in the morning, so if you could be downstairs ready to go at nine, that would give me plenty of time to go over everything with you."

"Sounds good."

He started to leave, then stopped and turned back around. "Also, no visitors allowed in the building unless they're approved first by me."

"That's kind of…stringent, isn't it?" Also, it was none of his business who I invited over.

Toly stood his ground. "I have to have a record of everyone coming through the warehouse. It's a security thing. Company policy."

"Okay, got it." I was supposed to be the happy new employee, not the difficult new employee, so what else could I say? Besides, I couldn't imagine what visitors I'd be having anyway.

"All right then." He waved and headed off. "You need anything, you let me know."

"Will do." As he headed back to the elevator, I unlocked the door and hauled my stuff in. I got the door shut, dropped my bags, then looked around.

As free, one-bedroom apartments went, it was nice. Really nice. Hardwood floors, granite counters in the kitchen that was part of the big open living room/dining room setup, and sleek, modern cabinets. I walked through another door and saw a big bedroom with a walk-in closet and full bathroom, also with a granite countertop.

And a large soaking tub.

Okay, this place was exceptionally nice. And it was included as part of the deal for working at the shop. I had to assume the rest of the apartments were similar. After all, Toly didn't know I was North Pole royalty. I'd been given this apartment based on being Lilibeth Holiday, not Jayne Frost.

You'd have to have some pretty strong motivation to walk away from a place like this. If another company was poaching the shop's employees, they had to be offering up a significantly cushy deal. But poaching alone wouldn't cause North Pole citizens to disappear altogether. Something else was going on. Obviously.

Unless they were being poached to join some super-secret shadow agency of supernaturals. Or maybe I'd been watching too many superhero movies.

The place was fully furnished with everything necessary, from what I could see. A leather sofa with a matching side chair, a flat-screen TV, dining table and four chairs, all the good stuff. I checked the kitchen cabinets. More than enough pots, pans, bowls and plates for a girl to cook up a storm, if she wanted. My cooking mostly consisted of warming up frozen pizzas and microwaving Hungry Man TV dinners. Yes, Hungry Man. Because there was no Hungry Elf brand. Which would probably just be an assortment of pies and cobblers. Also, I could heat up soup like nobody's business.

But what I needed to do right now was get unpacked and check in with my dad. Time to see if the snow globe had survived the trip and if it was really going to work. I rolled my big bag into the bedroom, hoisted it onto the bed and unzipped it.

The snow globe was in a box, swathed in bubble wrap and totally in one piece. I unwrapped it and sat cross-legged on the bed, then gave it a shake.

The snow swirled in a mesmerizing way. I stared into it, losing myself in thoughts of home. Did anyone miss me outside of my family? Probably not. My dad had come up with the cover story that I was taking a break from monitoring the N & N list to help my mother inventory our personal Christmas decorations.

It was a good cover. Our Christmas paraphernalia was housed in two separate outbuildings on some back acreage of my parents' property (technically the Winter Palace). It would take weeks to inventory that much stuff. When the Winter Palace was done up for the season, there was no mistaking that Christmas was on its way.

My dad's face appeared in the snow. "You made it. How was your trip?"

I could see from his surroundings that he was in the palace living room. "Good. Long."

"I'm sure you're tired."

"Not too bad. I slept part of the way. But I also memorized the dossier you gave me."

My mom peeked over his shoulder. "Hi, honey. How's Nocturne Falls?"

"So far so good. I found a place that has great pie. Not as good as yours, but it'll do until I get home."

She waved. "Love you. Miss you. Take care of yourself."

I waved back. "Thanks, Mom."

She disappeared, and my dad took over again. "I know it's early days yet, but have you learned anything?"

"Nothing much. I met Toly. He's exactly like what I thought he'd be; a true tinker. I start work tomorrow."

My father nodded. "Good."

"Hey, is it really company policy that all visitors have to be registered?"

He frowned. "I'm not sure. I can find out."

"Please. I'd like to know. Also, are all the employee apartments this nice?"

"It's been a while since I've seen them, but they should be."

I looked around at the room. "I can't imagine another company could beat this deal."

"Neither can we." He leaned in a little. "If you need anything, let me know."

"I will. I'm sure I'll be fine. My only need right now is to find the closest grocery store and get some food for the week. Other than that, I think I'm set."

"All right. Take care, Jay. Love you."

"Thanks, Dad. Love you too."

His image disappeared. I started to put the globe on my nightstand then thought better of it. I carried it out through the bedroom and into the living room, where I set it on a side table. That way

I'd pass it every morning. And it wasn't anywhere too personal, just in case.

I opened the fridge and freezer to see if there was any sort of welcome food package, but there wasn't. No big deal. I used my phone to look up the closest grocery store. The Shop-n-Save was about a twenty-minute walk.

That would give me a chance to see some of the town and learn where things were. Not bad.

I grabbed my keys and my purse and headed out. I could unpack later. Food, on the other hand, was a priority. No elf could survive long without a proper intake of vitamins and minerals.

Just kidding. The only real nutrition info I was interested in was how many grams of sugar the item contained. And in my case, the more the better.

I lugged my groceries back in three reusable bags that I bought at the store after realizing I'd filled the conveyer belt with more stuff than could easily be carried in paper or plastic. I put the bags down outside my door to open it, and as I was digging in my purse for my keys, I heard crying.

Animal crying.

I went still and listened. It sounded feline and close and a little feeble. I followed the noise to the apartment next to mine. As I approached, the sound got more insistent and was accompanied by scratching.

I grimaced. "Kitty? You okay?"

The cries turned to honest-to-goodness caterwauling, which I took to mean that the cat wasn't okay. "Hey, settle down in there. Your owner is going to get mad at me."

Yeah, that helped. More crying ensued. I

glanced toward the elevator. The cat's owner must be working their shift right now. I wasn't about to meet one of my new co-workers by heading down there and telling them their cat was having issues.

I'd never had a cat. Maybe crying like a newborn was what they did, but the poor animal seemed to be in real distress. "Okay, hang on, kitty cat. I'll be right back."

I hustled my groceries into my apartment then ran back into the hall. None of my neighbors seemed to be bothered by the cat's crying, so they were either all working in the shop or heartless.

Until I got to know them, I'd go with working. I put my hand on the door. "I'm back, kitty."

More scratching at the door. What I was about to do would not go over very well if whoever lived in this apartment found out, but hopefully that wouldn't happen.

I used one of the skills I'd inherited from my mother's side of the family; my ability to enter a residence without an actual access point. Chimney or no chimney. All I needed was a break in the structure, like where a door closed or a window met the sill.

A shimmer of magic, a moment where the weird, compressed feeling left me with a modicum of nausea, and I was standing on the other side of the door blinking away the urge to upchuck. I don't know how Uncle Kris did that all night long on

Christmas Eve. It made me feel hungover instantly. But I guess you got used to it.

Something rubbed against my leg. I looked down and saw a skinny, black cat. "Hey, dude. Are you okay?"

The animal was wearing a red collar with a silver disc hanging off it. I bent down (which did not help the nausea) and checked the tag. It took a moment for my eyes to focus, but I managed to read it. I looked at the cat. "Your name is Spider?"

He (Spider sounded like a boy's name) trilled at me, so I took that for a yes. Then he cried again, a long plaintive wail that dug into my heart.

"What's the matter, little man?"

He trotted off toward the kitchen. I stood and bit my lip. I'd only come to check on him, not traipse through a co-worker's place. But there seemed to be no one home.

I went after Spider and found him standing in front of two dishes. One was empty and one had a small puddle of stale-looking water in it. Whoever owned this cat wasn't taking very good care of him. "Okay, you're hungry. And probably thirsty, huh?"

I gave the water dish a good rinse, then filled it and put it back. Spider started drinking immediately. "Wow. You needed that."

On second glance, the apartment looked more than unoccupied. It felt abandoned. There was a fine layer of dust on the surfaces and a mustiness to the air. A hunch made me open the trash can lid. A paper plate lay on top of the garbage. It held the crusts of a sandwich, and the bread was speckled with mold.

How long had this poor cat been in here by himself?

Spider looked up from his water dish and meowed. He was still hungry. I glanced at a stack of mail on the counter and checked the name. Bertie Springle. The last employee to quit. Poor cat. Unless whoever lived here was holding Bertie's mail, Spider's owner wasn't ever coming back.

I took a quick stroll through the apartment. Other than the dust and staleness, it looked like someone had just stepped out.

Weird.

Twenty minutes later, Spider, his bowls, his toys, his bed, his litter box, and the bag of dry food I'd found were in my apartment and I was back on the globe with my dad.

"What's up? Find out something already?"

"Sort of. Can you confirm that Bertie Springle was in apartment 2C? His dossier doesn't list that info."

"I have that file in my office. Give me a moment."

I waited, watching parts of the house go by as he carried the globe into his office. He set the globe at the front of his desk, found the file, and flipped through it.

He looked up. "Yep. Bertie Springle. 2C."

"The last one to go missing. How long ago did he disappear?"

My father glanced at the file again. "Five days."

"Wow." Spider was in the kitchen, still chowing down. My heart twanged at the thought of him all alone in that apartment with nothing to eat. "No wonder his poor cat was so hungry."

"What?"

I explained to my dad about Spider and the apartment. "I'll keep him in case Bertie shows up, but don't you think it's odd that he'd leave his pet behind if he was just changing jobs? Actually, it's odd anyone would leave a pet behind for any reason."

"Very." My dad's brows pulled together. "Anything else odd?"

"There's a lot of stuff still in that apartment. Clothes, mail, personal stuff. That's all strange to me. No one moves without taking their things."

He nodded. "Not generally, no."

"Did anyone else leave their possessions behind?"

"We don't have any records on that, just who quit, when, and the note they left."

"Any chance the notes are forged?"

"No. We had the handwriting matched to samples in their files."

"So much for that idea." I sighed. "It's weird.

Almost like...I don't know, he left without knowing he was going to leave." Except for the note.

"That doesn't sound good." He frowned. "Be careful, Jay."

"I won't do anything stupid, Dad."

"I'm not worried about what you might do so much as what whoever's behind this might do once you start poking around."

"I'll stay in touch. And watch my back."

He smiled a little reluctantly. "Do you remember any of those self-defense lessons?"

"Some." I'd taken the class only because my mother had thought it was a good idea before I went off to college. "But I'm not going to need them." I wouldn't. My magical powers packed a much bigger punch.

"I hope not. Don't be afraid to use the full extent of your magic if need be."

"I won't. Talk to you soon." I pushed the button on the back of the globe and ended the conversation. I'd been here for only a few hours. I wasn't ready to get called home just yet because my dad thought I was in danger.

I sat back on the couch and put my feet on the coffee table. This place was nicer than my North Pole digs. (No, I didn't live in the palace. I'm a grown woman. I have my own place.) And Nocturne Falls was considerably warmer.

Spider walked over, jumped onto the cushion next to me and settled in to clean himself.

The poor, sad baby. He must have been freaked out being alone so long. "Get enough to eat, little one?"

He stuck one leg into the air and licked the back of his thigh.

"Show-off." I scratched his head. He stopped licking long enough to lean in and enjoy the attention. "Bad news, Spider. Bertie's most likely not coming back. Good news is, you're welcome to stay with me as long as you like. Is that cool with you?"

He started purring. Good enough for me. And just like that, I had a cat. I gave him one more scratch then left him to his bath and got up to look out the window.

Huh. There was an old-fashioned fire escape out there. It was just enough to be a little balcony. Or sneak guests in. I laughed at the thought. Maybe I'd put a potted plant out there. Catnip for Spider. I could see myself sitting out there, catching some rays. You know, if I was actually going to be staying here.

I wouldn't be sitting out there now anyway. The sun had set, and from the small slice of Main Street I could see, the town looked to be getting busier. I knew I had work tomorrow first thing, but I suddenly wasn't the least bit tired. Napping on the plane combined with the time difference meant I was wide awake.

I should go out and meet some locals. See if I could pick up any chatter about other town residents mysteriously picking up and leaving. Maybe this wasn't happening only at Santa's Workshop.

Or maybe I should have one night of fun before the real work began.

Right after I unpacked. I knocked that out pretty quickly, using the time to make my plans for the evening. I decided to go with a night of fun seeing as how it could do double duty as a chance to research the town. Pleased with my own cleverness, I got ready.

The shower was a revelation of marble, glass, and double-headed sprayers that never ran out of hot water. Any lingering travel weariness went right down the drain. I was ready to get out and see Nocturne Falls at night.

Catching sight of myself in the mirror gave me a little shock. The bracelet I wore turned my long, deep blue hair to white blond, shortened my nose and turned it up at the end and made my gray eyes ice blue. My cheekbones seemed a little higher and my chin had a hint of a cleft. My ears looked pretty much the same. That was nice.

And while I was cute, I definitely wasn't the highly recognizable Winter Princess anymore. That was kind of fun. I could be whoever I wanted. People would no longer react to me because of my status.

But looking at myself like this made me feel like I was wearing a mask I couldn't take off. It was oddly claustrophobic. I decided to avoid mirrors as much as possible for the duration and just enjoy the side benefits of being a regular, non-royal elf.

That made my makeup application quick. I dried my hair, threw on a different pair of black jeans, a white T-shirt covered in small iridescent crystals, my old leather jacket, and boots. I didn't know where I was going, but I looked chillacious.

I did a runway walk through the living room. "What do you think, Spider?"

He was asleep, bless his little cat heart. Probably worn out from eating so much. Or worrying. He might have starved to death if I hadn't found him. On that note, I refilled his food dish to the top. I hoped he wouldn't wake up and think he'd been abandoned again, but leaving a note was kind of pointless.

I tucked some cash, my phone, and my Lilibeth Holiday credit card and ID in the inside pocket of my leather jacket and headed out.

On my way through the vestibule, I stopped in front of the elevator I wasn't supposed to touch. It only had one button.

I pushed it.

No response. Then I noticed the keycard reader

next to the button. No wonder it hadn't worked for me.

I could use my magic and slip through the crack of the doors, but if there wasn't a car waiting on the other side for me to materialize into, I would fall.

Not worth the risk.

I walked outside and was greeted with a beautiful April evening. I drifted onto Main Street, peering into shop windows and people watching. I got a couple of "nice ears" comments, but they weren't snarky.

Apparently, having pointed ears in this town was a plus.

I was hoping to find a spot crawling with supernaturals, which I guess made me a tourist of a different kind, but the best I could do was a local bar and grill called Howler's. I went in and found a seat at the bar. For a Tuesday, the place was decently busy.

As the pretty redheaded bartender approached, I knew I wasn't too far off the mark when it came to finding a place that catered to non-humans. She was some kind of supernatural. Elves can usually spot other supernaturals, but we don't have the skill set for determining what specific kind they are unless they're also elves.

She put a square napkin in front of me. "Welcome to Howler's, I'm Bridget. Would you like a menu or just something to drink?"

I hadn't been hungry until she brought up food. "I'll look at a menu. And I'll have a mojito. If you have those."

She smiled. "We do. Preference on the rum?"

"Whatever you think is good." The main drinks at the Pole were mulled wine, spiked eggnog and hard cider. I was ready for anything else. And how wrong could you go with rum, mint and sugar?

She handed me a menu from underneath the counter. "Be right back with that drink."

I perused the offerings, settled on lobster mac-n-cheese, and then took a look around. There were other supernaturals in the place, but there was a good mix of humans too. This definitely wasn't a supernaturals-only spot.

When she returned with the drink, I ordered the meal, but lowered my voice with my next question. "I'm new in town. Could you tell me if there's a place that's only for people like us?"

She glanced at my ears and smiled. "Let me guess. A friend of Willa's?"

None of the missing elves had been named Willa that I could remember. "Sorry, I don't know who that is. I'm a new hire at Santa's Workshop."

"Oh, elf, not fae. Got it. You want something a little more exclusive, try Insomnia. Just a sec." She grabbed another square napkin and jotted down an address. "I don't go there very often—too busy—but you have to be…one of us to get in."

I took the napkin and tucked it in with my phone and ID. "Thank you."

"Sure thing. Welcome to Nocturne Falls. Holler if you need anything else. I'm going to get your order in."

"Thanks, Bridget." I still didn't know what kind of supernatural she was, but she'd been kind and given me the info I'd wanted. While I waited on my food, I wondered if she knew anything about the missing elves. Bartenders were pretty connected. But then the place got busier and it didn't seem like the right time to ask those sorts of questions.

I ate the mac-n-cheese, which was really good, then called a Ryde to come get me. According to my phone, Insomnia was a few miles away and too much to walk. I paid my bill, thanked Bridget and went to the curb to wait.

My Ryde showed up a few minutes later, making me very thankful I'd signed up for the car service before coming here. I had a driver's license (Alaskan) but that was all for show and had been magically attained. I really had no idea how to operate a vehicle that wasn't a sleigh or snowmobile, and since this town was short on both, I was happy to let someone else drive.

I got in, sat back and tried not to fidget. Something told me it was going to be an interesting evening.

The Ryde driver pulled into a parking lot filled with high-end foreign sedans and a couple of higher-end sports cars, then rolled to a stop in front of a set of rusty double doors.

I squinted up through the SUV's window at the building attached to those doors. Faded paint spelled out the name Caldwell Manufacturing on the old brick structure that looked only slightly younger than Uncle Kris. This was taking the industrial thing to a whole new level. I leaned toward the driver. "Can you stick around until I poke my head inside?"

He nodded.

I jumped out and tried one of the rusty doors. It opened smoothly, not at all like it was on the verge of decaying off its hinges. But then all those cars in the lot had to belong to someone, right? So where were those people?

I went inside and figured out the answer on my own. Past the rows of machinery and worktables dusty with disuse, a buff dude in a black suit stood guard next to a shiny steel elevator. Had to be a doorman.

The odors of dust and grease accompanied the utter stillness of the place. I gave the doorman a little wave. "This is Insomnia, right? Bridget from Howler's sent me."

To my relief, he smiled. "You got the right place."

"Thanks. Let me tell my driver he can go." My driver. That sounded so fancy.

I gave the Ryde guy a thumbs up that all was well and headed back inside to the snazzy freight elevator and the built doorman. There was a keypad by the buttons, but maybe the doorman punched in the code. Or maybe he turned over the code once I forked over the price of admission. Hmm. I wondered if he had access to the restricted elevator in the warehouse. But now wasn't the time for that. "Is there a cover?"

He nodded. "Fifty."

That was a little steep. "No discount for women?" Even the clubs in the NP had ladies' night.

He smiled. "That is the discount."

"Got it." I reached into my jacket pocket, not sure I had that much cash on me. "Do you want to see ID too?"

"You smell like elf and your ears confirm it, so we're good there."

"I don't think I've ever been told I 'smell like elf' before. I hope that's a good thing."

His eyes took on a feral gold gleam. Probably shifter of some kind. "It's not a bad thing."

Was he flirting with me? That was...new. And sort of fun. I pulled out the wad of cash I'd tucked in my pocket. I had two tens, a five and a couple singles. So much for covering the cover charge, but that's all I'd had in my wallet. I should have asked my dad for some petty cash before I'd left. I sighed. "I don't have enough cash for the cover. Do you take credit cards?"

"Put her on my account."

I almost jumped. The voice had come out of nowhere. And what a nice voice it was, sort of softly Irish and a little gravelly.

The doorman stiffened, his nod as respectful as a nod could be. "Done, Mr. Garrett."

I turned to see who Mr. Garrett was.

My first guess was Johnny Depp's taller, cleaner cousin, but last I checked, Mr. Depp didn't have fangs. I didn't need to be hit with a snowball to know what that meant. Garrett was a vampire. And an incredibly gorgeous one at that.

He looked exactly like a vampire should look, as far as I was concerned. Lean and broody, his wavy, black hair curled around his face in little points to highlight the dusting of stubble covering his strong jaw, the hollows of his sculpted cheekbones, and his incredible piercing eyes. Tiny silver hoops hung from his ears, and his black dress shirt was unbuttoned more than was civil, allowing silver chains and the pale vee of his chest to peek out. The only spot of color on his outfit was the long ivory scarf hung around his neck, like he'd just escaped an insufferable opera.

I swallowed and found my voice. "Thank you."

He smiled, showing off those fangs a little more, and held out his hand. "My pleasure. Greyson Garrett, at your service. And you are?"

Mesmerized by a voice that sounds like silk drawn over steel and dusted with the lilt of the Irish. I reached to shake his hand, but he captured my fingers, turned my palm down and brought my knuckles to his mouth, brushing his warm lips over my skin while his eyes gleamed silver and arrowed into me.

Tendrils of heat curled through me, and my mind went blank with sensation. Was this some kind of vampire magic? He'd asked me a question, but I had no earthly idea what he'd said, just that he smelled like cinnamon. I knew it was wrong to want to lick someone I'd just met, but the urge was definitely present.

"Hi." I somehow kept my tongue in my mouth.

His grin widened. "Hello. Your name?"

Oh yeah. My name. Who was I again? "Lilibeth Holiday."

"Lilibeth." The way the word rolled off his tongue, I almost wished it was the name I actually answered to. "Shall we?"

He could have asked me to do just about anything right then, and I would have said yes. "Sure." In a genuine Christmas miracle, I remembered my manners. "And thank you again, that was very kind of you to take care of the cover for me. I have the money, just not on me. I'm happy to pay you back."

"I wouldn't dream of it." Greyson nodded at the bouncer. "Chet, if you would."

The doorman leaned over and punched a code into the keypad next to the elevator. The whirr of gears echoed through the warehouse, and the down button lit up blue.

When the doors opened, we stepped in, and Greyson pressed the only button on the panel. Fortunately it was a quick ride that required no small talk, but allowed me to enjoy his hotness close up. It didn't disappoint. When the doors reopened, I shifted my gaze to the club. My mouth fell open in wonder.

Insomnia was so cool it made the North Pole look steamy. I did my best not to gawk, but the place was gorgeous. Dark and moody, industrial and sleek, but lush at the same time. Leather seating, brushed metal accents, lots of blue neon, water features, floaty white drapery, and the occasion blast of a smoke machine.

"This place is like a dream."

Greyson stood at my side, nodding. "That's the idea, I suppose. Insomnia and all."

"Oh, right." Proximity to vampires apparently cost me some IQ points. How many more, I had no idea, but I was willing to risk it.

"Buy you a drink?" he asked.

"I should probably be buying you a drink."

"Perhaps. But I'm guessing you don't get the Nocturne Falls employee discount."

"You work for the town?" That was interesting.

"Sometimes." He tipped his head toward the bar as he started walking toward it. "Come."

And I did, following him to a cozy half-round booth on a side wall that offered a perfect spot for viewing most of the club. A reserved sign sat on the table, which he ignored.

I sat but gestured at the placard. "Is that for you then?"

He shrugged. "Sure."

I laughed. "I like your attitude."

"And I like you. There aren't many fae in town."

"I'm elven, not fae, but we get confused a lot."

"My apologies. An elf then. And I suppose you should know that I'm—"

"A vampire. I figured that out. The fangs were sort of a giveaway."

His mouth pursed into the most positively kissable shape. "I was going to say Roma. We were called gypsies in the old days. But that's not so popular a word anymore." He winked. "And also, yes, a vampire."

A server came to take our order. I got another mojito, while Greyson ordered whiskey.

I waited until the girl left then asked, "Why tell me you're Roma before telling me you're a vampire? And actually, I would have guessed Irish."

"I assumed you knew I was a vampire, but I told you I was Roma in case our magic isn't compatible. And I am Irish." He winked. "You can be both, you know."

I grinned. "So you have magic? Outside of being a vampire?"

"Oh yes." He leaned back, and his fingers went to a black leather cord entangled with the silver chains around his neck. "Quite a lot."

As someone who had quite a lot of magic myself, I was curious what his magic might be. I'd never thought of vampires as being more than that. "Show me."

He smiled and presented his hand as if asking for mine. "I can read your palm and tell your fortune."

I laid my hand in his, and his fingers curled around my wrist, touching the bracelet that was hiding my identity.

His eyes widened, and his grip tightened on my wrist. "You aren't who you say you are."

I did my best not to react. "Why would you say that?" I'd have never guessed Roma magic would supersede elf. I felt a little trapped.

His eyes narrowed. "I see another woman in your place."

I laughed it off and eased my arm away to show off my bracelet. "I think you touched my bracelet. You probably saw a woman with dark blue hair and gray eyes, right?"

He nodded, still looking unconvinced.

I smiled. "That was my friend Jayne." Close enough. "She gave me this bracelet and put a good luck charm in it." I figured he'd appreciate the good luck bit.

He stared at the bracelet, and then his face broke into a smile. "That's a good friend."

"We're very close." I guess he believed me, but he didn't seem eager to try telling my fortune again. Too bad. It had been a good excuse to hold hands. "What do you do for the town?"

"I fill in as the VOD a few times a week."

The server returned with our drinks, put them on the table then left again.

"What's the VOD?" I sipped my mojito. It was

really good. So good I was a little worried about how fast it might go down. Good thing I'd eaten.

"Vampire On Duty." He lifted his glass to mine. "Here's to new friends."

"New friends." I clinked my glass against his. "Then you're one of the characters who walks around and takes pictures with tourists?"

He nodded.

"But you're a real vampire."

"That's the beauty of living in this town. You can be yourself, and the tourists think it's part of the act."

"I'd heard that, but I guess I didn't really get what that meant." I poked at a piece of mint with my straw. "That explains why I got so many compliments on my ears."

His smile went sly. "They are exceptionally nice ears."

"Thanks." I blushed. Like, actual heat rose up in my cheeks. I pushed the drink away. I needed to focus. "I have another question for you." Anything to change the subject.

"Sure."

"Do you know the toy store in town, Santa's Workshop?"

"Yes. You work there, right?"

"How did you know that?"

"They only hire elves."

"Oh. Right. So do you know the elevator that's

part of that building? The one for town employees only?"

"I do."

"Where does that go?"

He smirked. "You ask a lot of questions."

"I'm a curious sort." I did my best lash fluttering in hopes of a real answer. "So where does it go?"

He laughed, a nice deep chuckle. "I can't tell you."

Which meant he did know. "Or you'd have to kill me?" My smile froze, then melted off my face. That probably wasn't a good thing to say to a vampire.

He shook his head slowly. "Or I'd have to explain to the Ellinghams why I violated the non-disclosure agreement I signed prior to my employment." He squinted. "You don't honestly think vampires kill people, do you?"

I shrugged sort of noncommittally. "No. But you could, right?"

"Yes," he hissed. "And so could you."

I'd struck a nerve. I put my hands up. "I'm sorry. I didn't mean to upset you. You're the first vampire I've ever met. I don't know much about any other kind of supernatural besides elves. Except for college and some trips here and there, I've pretty much lived my whole life at the North Pole."

His brows shot up, accompanying his look of

disbelief. "As in the North Pole at the top of the world?"

"Yes. No. Sort of. It's the magical North Pole. You can't really get there unless you're a winter elf and have…clearance." Like flying reindeer. Or you knew where one of the portals was.

His good mood returned. "You're forgiven. I suppose you have more questions about vampires then?"

I did, actually, but I liked Greyson. I didn't want to wear out my welcome with him. "It's okay. We can talk about something else."

He nodded. "You're a winter elf then. See? I'm learning too. What does it mean to be a winter elf?"

I lifted my hand, aimed my fingers at him, and sent a small flurry of snowflakes in his direction.

He laughed again, louder this time, and sat up straight. "That's very impressive. What else can you do?"

I could fill the whole place with snow, freeze him solid, shoot icicles like bullets, and all sorts of other things. But I was Lilibeth Holiday, average winter elf, not Jayne Frost, exceptionally talented winter elf and heir to the winter throne. I had to cool it. Pun intended. "That's about it. Unless you'd like your drink chilled a little more."

He wiggled the glass back and forth, rolling the spherical ice cube against the sides. "I'm good for now, thanks."

"What other kinds of supernaturals live here?"

"All kinds. Name one, I'm sure they're represented."

"That's crazy. In a good way." I scanned the club, studying the faces. "And everyone in here is a supernatural, right?"

"Right. Unless someone's brought a human guest, but that's rare."

I sipped my mojito. No point in letting good rum go to waste. "What was the doorman then?"

"Chet's a black bear."

"Get out." I leaned in. "Are there werewolves too?"

Greyson laughed. "Oh, yes. And witches and fae and gargoyles."

"Wow." I couldn't believe it. Obviously, I'd known what kind of town Nocturne Falls was, but man, had I underestimated it. No wonder my father was afraid I wouldn't want to come back. This place was turning out to be far more interesting than the North Pole. "Who's a werewolf in here?"

"Didn't you say you went to Howler's before coming here?"

"I did."

"The woman who owns the place is a werewolf. She's usually behind the bar when she's not in her office so you may have seen her."

"Bridget?"

"That's her."

"She waited on me! I sat at the bar. I knew she was *something*, I just didn't know what. How cool." I stared out at the people on the dance floor.

"You want to join them?"

I looked at him. "You mean dance?"

He nodded. "Much better view from there too."

A little spark of joy lit inside me. "I'm in."

We spent the next hour (or two?) dancing while Greyson simultaneously pointed out various supernaturals in the crowd around us and explained who they were and what jobs, if any, they did in town. It was quite the education.

Finally, we took a break, went back to the table, and ordered another round. Dancing had made me thirsty, so the first half of that mojito went down fast.

In fact, I was almost done with it when Greyson's gaze latched on to someone in the crowd. He looked over at me. "If you'll excuse me, I see someone I need to talk to."

"Sure. I should go anyway." As soon as I sucked down the last of the drink. "Tomorrow is my first official day on the job and all that." All that being figuring out why Santa's Workshop's workers were disappearing while, at the same, being a good employee. That would require some sleep. And no more mojitos. Plus, Spider was waiting on me.

Greyson stood. "I didn't mean for you to go. I won't be long."

"Thanks, but I really do need to go. It's getting

late. This has been awesome. I really appreciate the company and the cover charge. And the education." I pulled some of the cash out of my jacket and laid it on the table.

He shook his head. "Don't even try that. Your money is no good to me."

"Very kind of you." I put the money away and slid out of the booth to stand next to him.

Then he leaned against the table, and his eyes took on the silver sheen I'd seen upstairs. "What if I want to see you again?"

That gave me a slightly-embarrassing, girlish thrill. I really needed to get out more. "Do you?"

"Yes."

We were eye to eye, so long as he stayed leaning. I smiled and decided to play it chill. "You know where I work."

"Until next time then, Lilibeth." He kissed my cheek, giving me another delicious whiff of his cinnamon scent.

The kiss was both chaste and devilish. It lingered too long to be classified as nice, but his mouth never moved lower than my cheek, so it wasn't exactly naughty either. For someone well versed in naughty versus nice, I was confounded.

And a little hot.

"Night," I muttered and took off for the elevator. Thankfully, the doors slid open as soon as I hit the button.

Chet the bear was still guarding the entrance. Now that I knew what he was, I could see it. Sort of.

"Have fun?" he asked.

"I did. I'll be back." No clue when, but why not? Insomnia was a happening place. Maybe I'd come back to celebrate achieving my mission. Then I could be Jayne and really let my hair down.

But for tonight, Lilibeth was going to bed.

I woke up unable to move my head and had a small panic attack until I realized Spider was sleeping on my hair. I slid him to a free spot on the pillow then gave him a scratch. "Morning, Spidey-cat."

He rolled upside down and stretched his paws adorably toward my face. He was seriously the cutest thing ever. Then he yawned and sent a stinky wave of cat breath in my direction.

"Oh, Spider, your breath is heinous." Mine probably wasn't much better. I hoisted myself to a sitting position and rubbed my eyes. I'd only had three drinks last night, but apparently the stuff they served at the Pole was watered down compared to real drinks or something, because I was feeling it.

Or maybe what I was feeling was a night spent dreaming about Mr. Garrett and his nice, naughty kiss. How had he turned such a sweet thing into a moment that had filled my dreams with so many wicked images? Roma magic? Vampire magic? Who knew?

I barely remembered getting ready for bed. I pulled my hair off my face, and something brushed my hand. I still had an earring in my left ear. The other one was probably in the covers somewhere.

Oh boy, I was not fully functioning.

An ice-cold, fully caffeinated Dr Pepper would help. I hoped.

I stumbled through the living room and into the kitchen and opened the fridge. Spider traipsed in after me, looking as bright and happy as could be, the tuna-breathed bugger. I squinted at the light as I grabbed a bottle of the good stuff. It wasn't quite as cold as I liked it. I turned the fridge temp down then wrapped my hand around the bottle. A quick blast of my magic and ice crystals formed in the liquid. Perfect. I leaned against the counter, twisted off the top and took a long pull.

Spider sat by his bowl, staring up at me, and meowed.

"I'm sure that means breakfast, right? I'm on it." I changed his water, then filled his other dish with dry food. The bag was almost empty. I'd have to get him some more, but I wasn't going to have time to hit the Shop-n-Save until my shift was over today. And I had no idea when that would be.

But I started at nine, which meant I had less than an hour to make myself presentable and get downstairs.

I showered, did the hair and makeup thing, dressed, ate a large bowl of frosted chocolate sugar crunchies, and drank as much Dr Pepper as I could manage. I was about to head down when I remembered Toly saying the housekeeping service came today. Since Spider had been Bertie's cat, the service must know not to let him out. He'd probably run and hide anyway as soon as he heard the vacuum. I assumed he'd be okay.

But I wasn't taking any chances with the snow globe. I tucked it away in one of my suitcases that was stowed in the walk-in closet.

Satisfied, I grabbed my purse and gave Spider a goodbye pat on the head. I walked through the shop's employee entrance at eight fifty-nine.

Toly was sitting on a stool behind the cash register reading the Tombstone, which I took to be the local paper. He lifted his head and smiled at me. "Morning, Lilibeth. Ready to get going?"

"Absolutely." *Not.* But I sounded enthusiastic, and that's what mattered.

"You can put your pocketbook behind the counter here."

"All right." I leaned in and stuck my purse in one of the cubbies.

He hopped off the stool, put the paper away and

presented me with a folded green square of fabric that had been sitting on the counter. "Put this apron on, and you're officially an employee."

"Thanks." I shook it out, slid it over my head and tied the strings behind my back. As uniforms went, it was pretty benign. And it had pockets, which was a plus.

I did a little pose. "How do I look?"

He chuckled. "Very nice, very nice."

I straightened and clasped my hands in front of me. "So what's first?"

"We'll start with a quick tour through the shop, then the warehouse. Juniper is on shift today from ten until five, so I'll have her show you the register, but for the first few hours this morning, I'd like you to do some stocking. It'll help you get to know our system and where things are on the shelves."

"Great. Lead the way."

And he did. In forty-five minutes, he'd shown me every toy in the store and explained where each was shelved and why, for what age group it was designed, and the kinds of children who'd most likely enjoy it.

If my head was aching before, it was throbbing now, but this time it was because of an overload of information, not tasty, tasty rum. This pretending to be an employee was going to be a lot harder than I'd anticipated. I nodded and smiled and did my best to look like it was clicking. It wasn't. Not all of it anyway.

I made a few attempts at asking about the missing employees, but Toly was having none of it. He was fully focused on teaching me about the warehouse and the store. Or maybe he was using that as an excuse not to answer. Either way, I got nowhere on that subject.

Then another worker showed up, and I got a reprieve from Santa's Workshop 101.

Toly introduced us. "Juniper, this is Lilibeth. She's our new hire."

Juniper was five feet of winter elf firecracker. Her short violet curls sprang off her head like they were trying to escape. She stuck out her hand. "Nice to meet you, Lilibeth. We sure can use the help."

"Well, here I am." I shook her hand. She had a grip like a stevedore. If she was happy for the help, did that mean she was unhappy about the workers who'd left? Maybe she knew something. I needed to talk to her more, but not with Toly watching.

He patted his stomach. "Juniper, you can teach Lilibeth the cash register after lunch. This morning I'm going to have her restocking."

"You got it, Toly." Juniper put on her apron, and as soon as Toly turned around, she stuck her tongue out and made crazy eyes.

I bit my lip to keep from snorting. Oh, I liked

this woman. And I was starting to wonder if Toly was maybe a little bit of a slave driver. Sure, he was a legend, but that was all about his inventions and toy innovations. Being a legend indicated nothing about his people skills.

I wasn't sure about the slave driver part yet, but he was *very* thorough. The tour continued through the warehouse and included a detailed description of what every shelf held, where new inventory was brought in, and how the Santa Bag worked.

Maybe I shouldn't have, but I stopped him there. I knew how the bag worked. Every elf who lived at the Pole did. It was one of the most widely known magical creations that came out of the NP, but also the most secret. It was basically a direct portal from the NP to wherever the bag was. I also knew every store had one, enabling them to get whatever stock they needed, whenever they needed it. Other stuff could be sent through it, but nothing living. Otherwise, I could have saved myself eighteen hours in coach.

And of course, the big man had the original Santa's Bag. Hence the name. How else do you think he delivers that many toys to that many houses? The bag gets refilled after every couple of stops.

It was a good system. Actually, it was a great system. Uncle Kris invented it himself, but then, he was the head tinker. And I didn't need Toly to give me a twenty-minute lecture on how it worked.

Toly ignored my interruption and finished his spiel about the bag anyway, making me wonder if he was dense or just stubborn.

An hour later, the tour was over and I was on the floor, literally, stocking the bottom shelf in the puzzle and game department. I was supposed to be checking SKUs and moving the oldest inventory to the front, but frankly, my desire to be employee of the month was non-existent.

And what was Toly going to do? Fire me? I guess he could, but—

"Excuse me, I need some help."

At the sound of the pleasant male voice, I looked straight into the legs of a man in uniform. Be still my heart. I followed the navy blue pants up to a utility belt and zeroed in on the firefighter's patch on the guy's sleeve.

Firefighters were hot. No pun intended.

My interest screeched to a halt at his face. The guy was a summer elf. Summer elves are those disgustingly flawless, California-types that are perpetually tan, have natural sun-kissed highlights in their perfectly tousled dirty-blond hair, and sport the kind of smiles that toothpaste companies rode to fame and fortune.

This guy was built like Disney's idea of a surfer. Tall with broad shoulders that tapered to a ridiculous vee at the waist, then right back out again at the thighs. He was muscle-y in that easy, ropy sort of way that implies a lot of outdoor activities as opposed to time in a stinky old gym. If that wasn't enough, he had a jawline that could shelter a small nation, blue eyes the exact color of a cloudless June sky, and a tiny, crescent-moon birthmark on his very firm right butt cheek.

That part I knew because this wasn't just any summer elf, this was Cooper freaking Sullivan, my ex-boyfriend from college. And the biggest mistake of my life. The iceberg to my Titanic, if you will.

The years since college had been kind to him, sharpening the edges of a face that had once held a lot of boyishness and turning him into something far more manly. Because that's what Cooper needed. To be more manly.

As if.

What were the odds of us ending up in the same town? "Cooper," I muttered.

His brows lifted. "What was that?"

Snowballs. I remembered the bracelet. He didn't know who I was. I stood up, brushed myself off and forced a smile. "I said super! What can I help you with?" *How about a nice kick in the babymaker? Huh? How about we start there?*

"Great. I need some toys."

Apparently, becoming manlier had made him dumber. "You're in the right place."

"Yeah, I guess I am," he laughed. Oh, that laugh. It sent a tingle right down into my girly-parts. Traitorous, wanton girly-parts.

My new goal was to make this as quick as possible. I checked his hands. No wedding ring. Didn't mean he wasn't married. *Focus*. "What kind of toys?"

"The station is doing some raffle baskets for the Nocturne Falls Elementary School fundraising dinner this Friday night, and I'm in charge of getting some toys to fill them."

That was not going to be quick. I glanced over at Juniper, but she was busy at the register. And Toly was at lunch.

And this *was* technically my job. Fake smile still firmly in place, I grabbed one of the big canvas shopping totes the store provided and looked Cooper square in the face. "Okay, great, let's get started."

"Awesome. I'll be back after lunch to pick the stuff up and pay for it."

"You're leaving?"

He stuck his hands in his pockets and rocked back on his heels. "Sure, we do these baskets every couple of months, and it's the same thing every time. I put my order in, one of you fills it for me, then I pay. Well, the station pays. But you know what I mean."

As much as I wanted him to go, I also didn't

want to get this wrong and give Toly a reason to reprimand me. "I don't know your budget, or what kinds of kids these are, or the types of toys they might like, or—"

"You're new here, aren't you?"

"Yes!" That might have come out a little louder than intended. "And I could use a little direction."

"Hundred bucks a basket. One for boys, one for girls, that sort of thing. Age range is elementary school, and educational stuff goes over big with the parents. And they're the ones who do the bidding, so we like to make them happy. Cool?" Then he leaned forward, and the stupid scent of all summer elves, a vague coconut suntan-oil smell, wafted over me, bringing with it a whole blizzard of memories. "Or would you like me to help you so you can go to lunch *with* me?"

Now that was the Cooper I knew. Super flirty, over-confident and completely full of himself. But he was a fireman in this town, and I'm guessing that made him pretty connected, so I couldn't really afford to muck this up. He might be useful at some point. Plus, I was getting good at fake smiling for his benefit. "As fun as that sounds, I only get twenty minutes for lunch, and I don't think I'm supposed to leave. Not on my first day. I'm sure I can pull this order together."

"You're sure?"

"Absolutely. You go enjoy your lunch…" I made

a show of peering at his name badge. "Fireman Sullivan."

He grinned. "You can call me Cooper."

I could think of a lot of other names I liked better. *Fake smile fake smile fake smile.* "Okay, then, Cooper. See you after lunch."

He left, and I'm pretty sure he made finger guns at Juniper on the way out. Or maybe he just waved. Whatever. I was actually happy he'd left. Having to spend more time with my ex than I already had wasn't something I wanted to do.

Summer elves were the exact opposite of winter elves. Their powers went in the direction of fire and heat. Which made it pretty funny that Cooper had ended up as a fireman. He would have made a better arsonist. But I guess being fireproof was a big perk in his chosen profession.

Some people said the Vikings were descendants of the summer elves, but that sounded like a good PR job to me. Whatever. Vikings were dumb too.

By the time I pulled toys for the baskets and calculated the totals to make sure I hadn't exceeded the budget (which required several swap-outs), Juniper had gone to lunch and come back and was now showing me how to log my break on the computer. I was starving and in desperate need of another Dr Pepper. And a nap, but that wasn't happening.

Naturally, Cooper showed up at the register just as I was about to leave.

"Oh, good, a customer," Juniper said. "Hey, Cooper."

"Hey, Juni." He smiled at me. "And new salesgirl."

Juniper smiled back. "This is Lilibeth. Today's her first day."

He nodded. "So I heard. Nice to meet you, Lili."

"Lili*beth*." I smiled tersely.

Juniper looked at me. "Cooper's a friend of mine."

I bet he was. "How nice." But if Juniper liked him, I'd better cool it. "Always good to have a fireman on call, huh?"

She nodded. "Let's ring up this sale, then you can take your lunch."

More fake smiling ensued. "I'm your willing pupil." My stomach protested, but what could I do?

We rang Cooper's stuff up while he made small talk about the lunch he'd had at Mummy's Diner. I may have said something about pie. The register wasn't too hard, basically a touch screen setup that was remarkably similar to the inventory computers used at the Factory. (Those were all hardwired, which was the only way to guarantee them functioning in the NP.)

Finally his stuff was bagged. He whipped out

the fire station's credit card, and Juniper showed me how to run it. He signed the receipt and that was that.

"Thanks for your help, Lilibeth. I'm sure I'll be seeing you around. So long as you don't disappear like the rest of them."

I went on full alert. Was the problem with the shop's employees that widely known? Or did he know more about it because he was an elf too? Or friends with Juniper? A part of me died inside as I knew I was going to have to talk to him some more to figure it out. "Nope, I'm here for good."

"Nice to hear. Juni needs the help, don't ya?"

Juniper nodded. "That's for dang skippy."

"See ya." He left, bags in hand.

I sighed, glad he was gone but even happier that I was finally going on break. "I get twenty minutes, right?"

"Yep. You doing all right? You look tired."

I smiled and meant it this time. Her concern was sweet. "Just hungry. I'll be back in twenty."

"Okay."

I made it upstairs in record time. Spider was sprawled out on the bed, luxuriating in a sunbeam cutting across the duvet. I couldn't tell if the place had been cleaned yet or not, so I checked the trash. It was empty. And the bathroom smelled like lemon. Yep, the service had been here.

That was fast. But I guess there hadn't been much to do seeing as how I'd just moved in.

I tossed a Hungry Man meatloaf dinner in the microwave, grabbed a Dr Pepper and drank half of it on my way back to the bedroom. I retrieved the snow globe from the suitcase in the closet and brought it back out into the living room. I thought about checking in with my dad, but all I wanted to do was eat then sit in peace for a few minutes.

I drank the remainder of the soda while I was waiting on my lunch to finish heating up. Twenty minutes was not enough time. Spider came out from the bedroom, all loose-boned and sleepy-eyed. He blinked up at me and ran his pink tongue over his chops.

"Are you telling me to top off your bowl?" I looked. It was half-empty. I guess he was making up for all those days without. I refilled it, which left about two more refills in the bag. "Cat food just moved to priority status."

The microwave beeped. I took the food out and peeled the plastic back, releasing a cloud of steam. Way too hot to eat.

I waved my fingers over the top, chilling it down a bit. Then I devoured it, polishing off another half bottle of Dr Pepper in the process. I was starting to feel elf again.

Good thing too, because my break was over in six minutes. Just enough time to hit the little elf's room, brush my teeth and get back downstairs. Maybe workers were leaving because there wasn't enough time to eat a proper lunch. I knew not bothering to give notice and leaving all your stuff behind was a pretty extreme reaction, but hey, people did crazy things when they were hungry.

I made a mental note to tell my dad about the insufficient breaks when I checked in, even though I knew it wasn't enough of a motivation.

Juniper was still at the register when I got back. I tucked my purse away and reported for duty.

"Feel better?"

"Less like I'm going to die, yes."

She nodded. "I get hungry on the job all the time. You know how it is with this metabolism."

"That I do."

She shuffled closer. "If you need a little something..." She reached back into one of the cubbies and pulled out a metal cash box with a handwritten label on a strip of duct tape that said *feminine supplies*.

"Cool, but it's not that time of the—"

She opened the box. It was filled with candy bars.

I snorted. "Oh, *those* kinds of feminine supplies."

"Yeah, I had to label it like that because when I tried just keeping a bag of candy under the counter, Toly and Owen went through it on the first shift. Just you, me and Buttercup know about this."

"Buttercup?" Some elf names could be a bit much, but that was really pushing it.

Juniper rolled her eyes. "Don't give her any grief about it. Her mother was a big Princess Bride fan."

"No grief from me." Especially seeing as how I was an actual princess.

"Good. The only rule of the box is we all replenish the stock."

"Got it."

She gave me a stern look. "And no generic crap either."

"Wouldn't dream of it."

She broke into a smile. "I'm so glad you're here. I mean, Bertie was cool and all, but he was a little odd."

Just what I needed; a chance to talk about the missing elves. "Bertie. That's the guy I'm replacing?"

"Yep."

"So he was odd? How?"

"Maybe I shouldn't be saying this, but—" A customer came in. Juniper smiled and greeted the woman, waiting until she got deeper into the store to continue. "He was pretty hung up on how powerful he was. As if you couldn't be a high-magicked elf and still be fun. I felt like telling him to get over himself. You can't work in one of the stores unless you have a reasonable amount of power, just in case you have to help with the shimmer."

Shimmer was a term elves used sort of the way witches used *glamour*. In this case, Juniper was probably referring to the frost on the windows and icicles on the eaves. "Really? I thought that was the manager's job."

"It is, and Toly does it, but once a week we do Snowy Saturday and that's a little bit more intense so he likes to know there's back up. Plus, sometimes he'll ask an employee to handle it so he can have a break. It's no big deal. If you've got the skills."

"Snowy Saturday?" I'd never heard of it, and I was pretty sure if the company had mandated it, I would have. I'd be checking with my dad all the same.

"On Saturdays, we make it snow in the store, but it can't accumulate for obvious reasons, like damaged merchandise and customer safety. That, plus the normal shimmer wears on Toly sometimes, I guess. Anyway, like I said, it's no big deal since it's just one day a week. And it brings in a ton of customers, so we always make our quota."

"There's a quota?" I'd never heard about one before.

"Sure. Personally, I think that's why some of the elves have left. Plus, Toly can be a bear to work for. If you don't perform, you'll know it. He'll call you into his office and have a talk with you about your salesmanship and blah, blah, blah."

Add that to the list of stuff I didn't know. I kept going with the questions. "There's been a lot of turnover? That's unusual for these stores. How much turnover are we talking about?"

Juniper thought a moment. "I think five workers since I've been here."

"You ever get called in for a talk?"

"Just once, but I've noticed —"

Toly waddled out from the back room at the same time as a new batch of customers came in the front door.

"Dinner after our shift?" she asked.

"I'm in." There was no way I was missing the rest of this conversation or a night out with Juniper. I liked her a lot. Not that I was trying to replace Lark, but well, maybe I was a little. Was that so awful? I'm not ashamed to admit I was a little desperate for a friend, as sad as that was.

Yep, that's me. Princess Pathetic. Fortunately, Juniper had no idea. About either of those things.

At four fifty-five, I met Owen and Buttercup, who was pretty much the exact opposite of my mental image of someone with that name. Short, spikey blue-black hair, heavy black eyeliner and pierced ear tips, which made mine hurt in sympathy. But she was sweet and, just like Juniper, happy to have another female on staff.

Owen was nice, but quiet. And he blinked a lot.

At five p.m. our shift was over, so Juniper and I ditched our aprons and bolted for the elevator.

"I'm on two," she said as she pushed the call button. "So is Buttercup. Owen's in the other apartment upstairs next to Toly and across from the corporate digs. Which means you must be on two also."

"Yep. I wonder if you're across the hall from me." The doors slid back and we got on.

"You might have gotten Bertie's old place."

"No, I'm in 2D."

Her brows lifted. "How do you know which apartment Bertie was in?"

Snowballs. I thought for a second as the doors opened and we got out. "About that…" I gave her a quick rundown about hearing Spider crying, but told her I'd picked the lock. Telling her what I'd really done would reveal me as royal. Then I said I'd done some snooping while I was in there and figured out who lived there. I hoped that covered my slip.

"I'm glad you saved Spider." She seemed mostly convinced, but Juniper was sharp. I wasn't calling myself clear yet. "You can pick locks, huh?"

I shrugged. "Everybody has skills."

"Sure, but mine probably won't lead to me getting arrested."

"You'd be surprised."

She laughed. "Change and meet back here in fifteen?"

"Deal." Once in my place, I switched out of jeans into black leggings, a snug tunic top and my black boots. Then I grabbed the snow globe and gave it a shake as I carried it into the bathroom with me to touch up my makeup.

My dad showed up as I was adding some eyeliner. "Hi, sweetheart. How was your first day?"

"Good." Not counting the part that included Cooper Sullivan.

"Any news?"

"Nothing concrete. Toly's a bit of a task master."

"Is that your take or the opinion of the workers you've talked to?"

"Both." I put the eyeliner away and did a quick dusting of powder to get rid of the shine that had accumulated after a day in the store. "I hope to know more about the workers who've left after tonight."

"Why? What's going on tonight?"

"I'm going out to dinner with the woman I worked my shift with. She's really nice. Juniper Trembley. She was about to tell me something today, then we got interrupted with Toly and customers and couldn't finish our conversation." I ran a brush through my hair. "Anyway, we should be able to dig back in at dinner. I think she trusts me. Or is starting too."

"Sounds like you're doing very well."

"I'm trying. Do you know what Snowy Saturdays are?"

"No, what are they?"

"You pretty much answered that question." I gave him the same explanation Juniper had given me.

He thought for a moment. "That might explain why that store is so successful. I wonder if we should do that in all the stores. I'll have to talk to Kris about it, see what he thinks."

"Um, maybe wait until this is over? Otherwise Toly might wonder how you found out."

"Good point. All right, I'll talk to you tomorrow."

"Dad, wait. Did you find out about the visitor record?"

He nodded. "Yes. That's got to be Toly's rule. HR didn't have anything on that."

Hmm. Toly was a task master and a fibber. "Two more things then. How long are the lunch breaks supposed to be? Legally, I mean."

"I'd have to check Georgia laws. Each store is governed by the state it's in."

"There's no company policy on this? With the perks of housing and the cleaning service, I would think breaks would be covered too."

"I'll find out as soon as I can. Good enough?"

I could Google it, I supposed, but this way my dad got to help me. Which I think he liked. "Yes, thanks. Second thing. Is there a quota the store has to meet?"

He narrowed his eyes. "You mean like sales? Not that I'm aware of, but I'll check on that too."

"Cool. Love you."

"Love you too." His image vanished and the snow settled.

I put the globe back on the side table in the living room, grabbed my purse, gave Spider's tummy a little scratch since he was lying on his back on the sofa like a man with no shame, and went out into the hall.

Juniper was just stepping out of her apartment. "Ready to eat?"

"Is no ever an answer to that question?"

She grinned. "Let's go."

We headed for the elevator as I asked, "Where to?"

She pushed the button. "A place called Howler's. It's a little touristy, but very supernatural friendly, and get this, the owner is a werewolf."

I probably should have acted more surprised, but this was not new information to me, thanks to Greyson. Who hadn't tried to get in touch with me, I'd noticed. "Bridget, right?"

The doors opened and we got on.

Juniper looked a little shocked. "Yes. How did you know?"

"I ate there last night. She waited on me since I sat at the bar."

"Yeah, but how did you know she was a werewolf? Most elves can't figure that stuff out. Is that one of your powers? Because that would be cool."

"No, nothing so amazing. Someone told me. That's all."

The lift touched down. We got out and I gestured to the bikes. "Are we riding or walking?"

"I'd prefer to walk."

"Me too."

As we pushed through the vestibule door, Juniper stopped.

"Hang on." She opened her purse and started digging through it. "I think I forgot my credit card. I had it out to buy something online."

"You need to run back up?"

"Maybe…"

"What are you doing by that elevator?" a voice barked.

We both turned to look. Toly stood in the doorway to his office, his gaze pinning us.

Juniper sighed. "I'm just looking for something in my purse. I'm not touching the stupid elevator." She pulled her credit card out. "Got it. Let's go before he has a meltdown."

We pushed through the door and onto the street.

It was a beautiful night, but any warmer and I'd have to change out my boots for sandals. If I owned sandals. Which I did not. "He sure is touchy about that elevator."

"Yeah, I guess if there's an issue, the town will blame him, and then he'll get in trouble with corporate. I sort of get it, but we all know to leave it alone, and we're not kids. No one has any burning desire to take a ride in that thing."

I did. A little anyway. "Any idea where it goes?"

"Down?" She laughed. "Don't know, don't care."

I changed the subject since that one seemed

dead. "So, we're having dinner at a place run by a werewolf. That's not something you get to say every day."

Juniper nodded. "That's for sure. And the food there is good and not too expensive. Which I'm sure you saw. Plus, it's served in mass quantities. Which I'm sure you also saw."

I laughed. "I did, and I'm not ashamed to say I cleaned my plate."

Howler's wasn't a far walk so we got there a few minutes later. Thankfully, the dinner crowd hadn't really descended yet, and we snagged a booth. Those always felt more private to me, which was good, because Juniper and I needed to talk.

We settled in, got drinks, and placed our orders (the prime rib special for both of us and an appetizer of loaded potato skins to share). Juniper was really easy to hang out with. That was a little different than being with Lark. Truth be told, Lark was a touch high maintenance. But you overlooked that stuff in friends, right?

With the food on its way, I started the conversation. "How long have you worked at the shop?"

"Just shy of two years."

"You like it then?"

She nodded and sipped her Coke. "I do. It's a good job. I like working with people and this town is great."

That was for sure. "But?"

"But Toly can be—" She smirked. "I shouldn't be telling you this stuff. You just started. You're supposed to be in the honeymoon phase when everything is peachy."

I used the backstory I'd been given. "Hey, it took me a year on the waitlist to get here, but I'm not some Pollyanna who thinks everything is perfect. I want to know what I'm dealing with."

She sighed. "Toly can be a little odd. Lately more often than not. You saw how he was tonight." She shook her head. "I think it's his granddaughter, but he doesn't talk about it much. It's just what I've picked up from bits and pieces I've overheard."

This was getting interesting, but I wasn't sure it had anything to do with elves leaving the shop. "Like what?"

She leaned forward, her glass between her hands. "First of all, you have to know that he requested the manager's job when he retired, specifically so he could live in Nocturne Falls and be near his granddaughter. She runs a B&B here in town. She's the only family he's got, as far as I know. Or at least the only family he's still in contact with."

"Makes sense that he'd want to be near her, then." I drank some of my Dr Pepper. Elixir of life, that stuff.

"Sure. But about six months before I got here, her husband filed for divorce."

"So two and a half years ago." Which is when the workers started disappearing. But I couldn't make the connection between the two things. Yet.

"Yep. I have no idea what happened and probably never will, but now she's running the business by herself and having a hard time making a go of it. Or was. I haven't heard much about it lately."

"Having Toly here is probably a big help."

"Totally. But that's about the same time he started acting, I don't know, more serious? More stressed?"

"Makes sense, though, right? His granddaughter's having trouble, struggling. He's got to be upset by that."

Juniper nodded. "Absolutely, but he shouldn't be taking it out on us. Also, that's right around the same time corporate started pushing those Snowy Saturdays." She rolled her eyes. "Toly monitors whoever he puts in charge of it relentlessly to make sure they get the shimmer right."

The potato skins arrived, so we put the conversation on pause to nosh, resuming after we'd both downed our first one.

"You think he's under pressure from corporate too, then?"

"Yep. I'm sure his job isn't easy, not with the stresses of his granddaughter's stuff going on too, but there are days when you just don't want to be around him."

It occurred to me that I might be able to wrap this thing up sooner than anticipated if what Juniper was saying about Toly was true. And I had no reason to think otherwise. Maybe the missing workers had gotten fed up with the cranky old guy and bailed. But that wouldn't explain why Bertie had left all his stuff and sweetie-pants Spider behind. Unless Toly had fired him and taken away his keys so that Bertie couldn't get back in. That was a possibility. "Is that why workers have left?"

"Could be."

"You don't sound convinced."

"Well, they just stop showing up. You'd think if it was because of Toly, they'd file reports with HR or say something to someone, you know? They'd at least complain to the rest of us. Or threaten to leave."

"Did Bertie give any hints he was leaving?"

She shook her head. "Nope. There one day, gone the next."

"Nothing happened right before he left? No blowout with Toly, no personal issues, nothing? It's really weird to me that a guy would leave and not take his cat. Or any of his stuff. There were clothes in the closet, shoes on the floor, and mail on the counter. I don't know who moves and leaves everything."

Juniper squinted, half a potato skin in her hand. "That is really strange."

"Did the rest of them leave that way too?"

"Can't say. It's not like I went in any of their apartments, you criminal."

I laughed, almost choking on my last bite of cheesy, bacon-y potato goodness. "Hey, I wasn't accusing you of anything. But maybe you saw someone moving stuff?"

"Not that I remember. And I know the day Bertie left because I had to cover his shift."

"Speaking of Bertie, maybe I should have a look around his place again."

Her eyes lit up. "Can I come?"

"I don't know. What if we get caught? Better that only one of us gets in trouble." Actually, bringing her along would mean she'd figure out my lock picking abilities were limited to the simplest of locks.

"How about you go in and I stand guard?"

I snorted. "That won't look weird at all, you hanging out in the hall in front of an empty apartment." But clearly she wanted to come. And it could be a good bonding experience, securing her trust in me even more. "How about if I text you once I'm inside and the coast is clear?"

She grinned. "Cool."

Our food arrived, and we dug in. The conversation shifted to how good the food was and then silence as we devoured it. In a sadly short amount of time, we finished.

Juniper put her fork down and leaned back. "Now is probably not the right time to tell you they make a killer peach cobbler here."

I wiped the last of the steak juice off my face. "I think now is the perfect time. Want to share one?"

We looked at each other then both said, "Nah," at the same time. Laughing, we ordered two with ice cream when the server came to refill our drinks and check on how our dinner was. She cleared our plates and went to get our desserts, leaving us to savor the feast we'd just put down.

"Thanks for inviting me to join you for dinner."

"You're welcome," Juniper said. "You want to walk around town for a bit after? Or we could go down to DOA and get some drinks. Check out the local talent."

"I take it DOA is a bar?"

"Yep. Stands for Drinks On Arrival."

"Cute name, but why not stay here?"

A male presence stopped her from answering.

"Staying here sounds like a great idea." Cooper Sullivan slid into the booth next to me, all smiley and flirty like we'd asked him.

Juniper seemed happy enough to see him, giving him a sly look in return. "Why? Are you buying?"

"Sure, what do you want?"

For him to leave. But I smiled. And wished he was ugly. That would make ignoring him so much easier. "Nothing for me, thanks. I had a couple drinks last night and they were more than I could handle."

Juniper put her hand on the table between us. "Didn't you just get in yesterday?"

"Yes. So?"

"So you're not supposed to drink twenty-four hours after leaving a magical plane. Everybody knows that."

"They do?"

Cooper nodded. "Absolutely. It's like being jet lagged. But worse."

"Well, I didn't know that." But then most of my traveling was done with my parents for official business, and there wasn't much drinking involved in that. "Huh. Maybe I'll have a drink after all."

Cooper shrugged. "I'm happy to buy you one, but don't feel pressured."

I stared at him and his nice guy response. I had to remind myself again that he thought I was Lilibeth. If he knew who I really was, he might be acting differently. Make that *would* be acting differently. I looked over at my tablemate. "What are you having, Juniper?"

"Glass of whatever sweet wine they have."

I made a face. "You mean like mulled wine?"

"No, silly. Something like a moscato."

"I don't know." I was a little embarrassed to admit I'd never heard of it, but like I mentioned, bars in the NP had a fairly limited menu.

Our desserts arrived, buying me a little more time to decide.

Cooper closed his eyes and took a deep inhale. "Howler's peach cobbler. Just about the only dessert worth eating."

He'd always loved peaches. Summer elves loved fruit the way winter elves loved sweets.

He unfolded his lanky form and stood. "I'm gonna make a bar run and get those drinks while you two enjoy your cobbler. What do you say about that wine, Lilibeth?"

"I'll try it, I guess."

"Be right back." He left us alone again.

I lifted my brows as I sank my spoon into the cobbler's sugared crust. "Do you have a little crush on him or does he have a little crush on you?"

She snorted. "Neither. I mean, I know him pretty well and we hang out as part of a larger group, but we're just friends. He's not really my type." She devoured a piece of peach with a hunk of ice cream melting off it, gave a little satisfied sigh, then licked her lips. "I think his crush is on someone *else*."

"Oh, no. Not me."

Juniper nodded, looking as satisfied as Spider after a full bowl of kibble. "Oh yes, you."

"No, thanks." I tried to focus my attention on the best cobbler I'd ever eaten, but Juniper didn't seem ready to drop the subject of Fireman Sullivan.

She made an incredulous face. "Why not? He's the total package. Or don't you like handsome men with incredible bodies and honorable jobs?"

"Sure, as much as the next woman, but I can't be in a relationship." Not with him. Been there, done that, got the heartache.

"Why? Did you just get out of one?"

I sighed. I hated to lie to Juniper any more than I already was. Plus, there was that whole thing where Cooper's connections within the community might help me with my mission. That was reason enough for me not to completely shut him down just yet. "You really think he likes me?"

She nodded, grinning. "Yes. When he gets back, I'll give him a chance to prove it to you."

"Wait—"

Cooper returned, his big hands cradling two glasses of wine and a mug of beer. "Here you go. Two moscatos." He set all three down, handed Juniper and me our drinks, and took his seat beside me again.

For a moment, I had a flashback to college. A nice one. We'd often gone out to the little pub near the campus to watch whatever sports game was happening, and we'd always sat next to each other like this. Same side of the table or booth. Cooper liked it that way. Liked to have me close.

Until he'd had enough of dating the Winter King's daughter.

Cooper lifted his glass in a toast. I took my drink and raised it to meet the others. "Here's to new friends." He looked at me. "Cheers."

"Cheers," Juniper and I replied.

I sipped the wine. It was pretty delicious. "Juniper, you were right. This is good."

"Told you." But the twinkle in her eye wasn't about wine. She grabbed her purse. "Gotta hit the ladies' room. Be right back."

And just like that, Cooper and I were alone. Was that what she'd meant about giving him a chance to prove he liked me? Nervous energy trilled through me. I never thought I'd be alone with Cooper again. Or this close to him.

He turned to face me. "So how do you like Nocturne Falls?"

"I haven't seen much of it, but what I have has been pretty cool."

He nodded. "I might be able to get one of the guys from the station to show you around. If you want. Not trying to set you up or anything, just offering."

Not what I'd been expecting. And so much for Juniper's theory. Which I decided to test. "You mean you don't want to show me around yourself?"

He shrugged and stared at his beer. "Sure, I could. But right up front I should tell you I'm not looking for...you know, *anything*."

If he'd set my hair on fire I'd have been less surprised. "I wasn't really implying..."

He laughed, a little self-consciously. "It's not because you aren't pretty or anything like that. I just don't think...never mind. If you want to go out sometime, that would be fine. As friends, though."

"Right. As friends." Wait, what was I saying? Had I just agreed to a date with Cooper Sullivan that I had set myself up on?

I gave the side eye to the glass of wine in my hand. Maybe alcohol and I just didn't mix.

"Okay then." He sipped his beer. "You like sweets, right?"

"Is there a winter elf who doesn't?"

He smiled. "When do you work tomorrow?"

"Not until five. I have the evening shift."

"Perfect. I'll pick you up at eleven and give you the tour of the best places in town to stock up on the good stuff. We can even skip lunch and just eat like unsupervised children all day."

I laughed. I couldn't say no to an outing that was my own doing. And really, this wasn't a date. It was a friendly outing. We'd already agree to that. "I'll meet you by the warehouse door at eleven."

He clinked his glass to mine. "See you then."

And just like that, I had a date with Cooper Sullivan.

I was going to have to talk to my father about hazard pay.

After three glasses of moscato apiece, Juniper and I called it a night, thanked Cooper (who'd generously paid for all six of those drinks), and headed home. We were both a little buzzed, but it was a short walk.

And Cooper insisted on coming with us, gentleman that he was. That kind of behavior was both sweet and incredibly frustrating. I was determined not to like the guy, but he was making it more and more difficult.

Of course, that non-date I had with him tomorrow probably wasn't going to help matters either. Granted, I could always tell him who I really was. That would cool his jets.

It would also violate my directive. Unfortunately.

Fortunately, we were at our building. We thanked Cooper at the warehouse door, jumped in the elevator, and then said our goodbyes in the hall.

As soon as I locked the door behind me and turned on the entrance light, Spider met me with a loud meow.

"Crap." I still hadn't gone for cat food. I picked him up and gave him a little kiss on the head. "I'm new at being a cat mama and not doing a very good job of it. But I will go first thing tomorrow, I swear. I'll even get some treats."

He butted his head against my chin.

"I promise there's enough for dinner tonight and breakfast in the morning, okay? Don't hate me." I made a mental note to buy cat litter too. That was not something I could afford to run out of.

He started purring, clearly the forgiving sort.

I flipped on the kitchen light, set Spider on the counter (because really, who was going to tell me not to?), and jumped at the sight of a dark figure on the other side of the window.

A second later, I realized it was Greyson. That was one way to avoid putting a visitor on Toly's list.

Frowning, I went over and jimmied the window open. "You scared the snowflakes out of me. What are you doing on my fire escape?"

He pointed at Spider. "Were you talking to the cat?"

"That's not an answer."

He smiled, which made me temporarily forget the question. Stupid Irish-Roma vampire magic. "Aren't you going to invite me in?"

"Is that a vampire thing? Like you can't come in unless you're invited?"

He snorted. "You watch too much TV."

"Yes, you can come in." I walked away from the window and went back to getting Spider his dinner.

When I rounded the counter, Greyson was already standing on the other side of it. Unnerved by his speed and stealth, I jumped and almost spilled what little kibble was left. "You could make a little noise, you know. Wear a bell or something."

"My apologies."

I dumped food into Spider's bowl. "This can't be a thing, you showing up on my fire escape. I'm not a misunderstood high schooler looking for an immortal boyfriend to stalk me into loving him. Normal people call or text."

He popped a brow. "And I would have, had you given me your number."

"Oh. Yeah. Sorry."

Spider chowed down like his life depended on it. Apparently, having a vampire in the house didn't register on cat radar. At least not enough to dampen his appetite.

"I went by the shop, but you weren't there. I

didn't ask for you. I didn't want to start any undue rumors."

I smiled. "You mean like the new employee is already dating the hottest vampire in town?"

He laughed, his cheeks going the tiniest bit red, which was ridiculously adorable and slightly surprising. I hadn't known vampires could blush. "Something like that, yes."

Suddenly, I felt like I had the upper hand. He'd come to see me. "How did you know what apartment I live in?"

"I didn't. I was one flight up when I saw the light come on."

"So you were just hanging out, waiting?"

He nodded slowly and pursed his lips. "I guess that is kind of stalker-y."

"A little. You might want to get that looked into. See a therapist, that sort of thing."

He smirked. "I'll do that."

I leaned against the counter and crossed my arms. "What did you need to see me so badly about?"

"Two reasons." He reached into his pocket and held out a long, dangling silver earring. "I believe you lost this last night."

So that's where my other earring went. And here I'd thought it was still in the covers. "I didn't even know I'd lost one." Then I shook my head. "Stupid twenty-four-hour rule."

"What?"

"Nothing. It's an elf thing." I took the earring. "Thanks. My mom gave these to me. What was the second reason?"

"I was going to ask you if you wanted to go for dinner, but it's late now and you've obviously come from a meal and drinks so—"

"What do you mean, obviously? I'm a little buzzed, but I'm not drunk by any means."

He tapped the side of his nose. "I can smell wine and steak on you. If I'd had to guess based on the other scents lingering in your hair, you were at Howler's."

Color me impressed. "Are a vampire's senses really that good?"

"Was I right?"

"Spot-on. Wow. That's kind of cool. I would have said yes, by the way."

"To dinner?"

I nodded.

"Tomorrow night, perhaps."

"I can't. I work the evening shift tomorrow." Which meant I could sleep in. At least until I had to get ready for my non-date with Cooper. But I wasn't ready to give up on time with Greyson that easily. "I'm not tired and it's not that late. We could go for a walk. It's a beautiful night."

"It is. A walk would be nice."

Yes, it would. I grabbed my purse. "You don't

know any twenty-four-hour pet stores, do you?"

He made a curious face. "I can't say that I do. Why?"

"Spider is almost out of food."

"Ate the last fly, did he?"

"Hah hah."

He grinned. "The Shop-n-Save is open twenty-four hours now. Just started last month."

"And you wouldn't mind walking over there with me?"

His lingering smile was answer enough. "Not at all."

"Okay." I checked my watch. It was a few minutes after ten. "One small problem. The shop is closed and the manager could be on his way back to his apartment. We can't run into him in the elevator. I'm not supposed to have guests up here without prior approval."

Greyson's brows knit together. "That's rather strict, isn't it? You are an adult."

"I know. But the apartment is included in my wages, and I just work here, I don't make the rules. It's something about having a record of everyone who's been in the warehouse. There's a lot of proprietary stuff in there." Like the Santa Bag that all our inventory was shipped through. Although why I was defending Toly's rule, I had no idea. It was kind of like living in a dormitory. "Anyway, I have no idea when he'll be back in his apartment, so—"

"We don't need to take the elevator."

"We don't?"

He shook his head and walked back to the window. "Trust me?"

"I don't know." If he was going to bite me and drink my blood, we didn't need to leave the building for that. Heck, I'd already invited him in. That was opportunity enough. "Yeah, okay."

"Good." He pushed the window up and exited with a sort of grace I knew I would not be able to duplicate. More vampire magic, I suppose. He held his hand out to me. "Come on."

I looped my purse strap across my body and took his hand. A moment later, I stood on the fire escape with him. "What now?"

He closed the window and smiled. "Now, the fun part."

He leaped onto the railing as light as a cat. "Your turn."

"You have a weird idea of fun." I shook my head. "I can't do that." Okay, I could. Elves were pretty nimble. But that was a very thin railing and we were two stories up. So, no.

He held out his hand again. "I'll help."

Holding his hand did sort of sweeten the deal. "I don't know."

"I won't let you fall." He wiggled his fingers. "You said you trusted me."

Reluctantly, I took his hand. He lifted me like it

was nothing. Oh boy. I was standing on the railing. Getting vertigo. And a little nauseous. "I can't be up here. I feel like I'm going to—"

He lifted me into his arms like a baby and jumped.

"Son of a nutcracker!" I sucked in a shuddering breath and was about to scream when we landed as softly as a snowflake floating down to earth.

He put my feet back on the ground, but I didn't drift far from the circle of his arms. "I'm sorry if I frightened you. Your heart is pounding like a drum. Are you all right?"

It took a moment for the reality of what had just happened to register, my head being all cluttered with fear and the scent of cinnamon. I put my hand on my chest. My heart *was* going pretty fast. "Physically, yes. Mentally, I'm not so sure. How did you do that?"

He shrugged. "Vampire skills."

I narrowed my eyes at him. "You could have told me what you were going to do."

"Would you have agreed?"

"Probably not." Then I smiled. "That has to be one of the coolest things I've ever done. Well, been a part of. But seriously, next time, ask. Or I can't be responsible for my reaction."

He held his hands up and backed off. "I will. Promise." He gestured down the street. "To the Shop-n-Save then?"

"Yes." I glanced up at the fire escape we'd just jumped off of. "Seriously cool."

He laughed softly, and we started down the street on our mission to secure cat food and cat litter. Talk about things you don't expect to be doing with a vampire.

"About dinner..." He looked at me. "Maybe Saturday?"

"Why not Friday?" Although I was off both nights since I was scheduled for the day shift.

"I'm the VOD Friday night."

"Vampire On Duty, right?"

He nodded. "From six until midnight."

"I guess Saturday night would be good then."

He smirked. "You guess?"

"I still want to know where that elevator goes." Because that might explain why Toly was so wound up about it.

Greyson laughed. "You really are tenacious."

"Does that mean you're going to tell me?"

"No."

I sighed with great effort. "What's the big secret?"

He rolled his lips in for a moment as if suppressing more laughter. "Why do you want to know so badly?"

"Because Toly, the manager, the same guy who won't let any of us have visitors unless they're cleared with him first, freaks out every time we go near that elevator. And I'm dying to know what the big deal is."

Greyson sighed. "The big deal is it gives access to a restricted Nocturne Falls town area, and if something happens because one of you gets down there via that elevator, he's probably on the line with the Ellinghams. Not to mention whoever he'd have to report to in the company. I'm sure your upper management wouldn't be happy about it either."

"Yeah, that's what I figured. But I still want to know what's down there."

"And I still can't tell you."

"Maybe I can't make dinner on Saturday night…"

His eyes took on a darkly wicked glint. "And perhaps the next time I visit your shop, I'll ask for you by name, telling them all how I had to find you to return the earring you'd left behind after our evening together."

I laughed and gave him a little shove. "Fine. I'll stop asking about the elevator."

He nodded. "Thank you. If the occasion arises that I can tell you more, I will. You have my word."

That was something. "All right. Thanks." Then I decided to push in a different direction. "Do you know about the elves that have quit their jobs at the store? Well, quit might not be explaining it right. In the last two and a half years, six elves have just up and left. They wrote a note, left their stuff behind—at least one did—and just didn't show up for work. Here one day, gone the next."

He was silent a moment. Like he was thinking. "I've heard."

"How did you hear?"

He rolled his shoulders. "I'm a town employee. Word gets around when a business is having issues."

Interesting. "Because?"

"Because the Ellinghams don't like waves. At least not the kind that could affect the rest of the town."

"They sound as bad as Toly."

"Not at all." He shook his head. "They've worked hard to make this place what it is. A safe haven for supernaturals of all kinds. They have a tremendous amount invested here, and they have every right to defend what they've built. Are they perfect? No. What family is? But they're good people. Loyal. Generous. Protective of the citizens who call this place home."

"That puts things in a different light. I can imagine they wouldn't be happy about the problem with the employees then."

"No, not at all."

And they wouldn't be happy with Toly or the company if anyone who wasn't authorized made use of that elevator.

Hmm. What if the missing employees had the same curiosity about that elevator that I had? What if they had accessed it somehow and that's why they were gone? If the town could take away the building for a violation, could they also remove employees?

That might explain why Toly was so on edge about it—he was tired of workers who couldn't keep their mitts to themselves. "What's the Ellinghams take on the missing employees?"

He gave me a look I couldn't quite decipher. "I'm not sure I'm supposed to be talking to you about this."

I smiled sweetly and looped my arm through his. "But you already are."

The side of his mouth lifted in a reluctant half smile. "They're concerned, and they're monitoring the situation, but whoever runs the company that owns Santa's Workshop has been made aware that this issue needs to be resolved. That's all I know. And probably more than I should have said."

My gaze shifted straight ahead. Was that why I'd been sent? Because the ruling family of vampires had been in touch with my father about an issue that might impact their town? Or had my dad really just found out because of the census? Or had the two occurrences collided? I had a lot of questions to ask the next time I spoke to my dad.

"You look lost in thought." He jostled my arm a

little to get my attention. "If you're worried that something might happen to you because of what's happened to the other employees—"

"Worried is an interesting choice of words, isn't it? That sounds like something bad has happened to them." Which I didn't want to believe. "All I've heard is that they stopped coming to work."

"And left everything behind. You said that yourself."

"Just the one that I know of."

"Even so, why would someone leave everything behind unless they had no choice? What kind of situation would you have to be in to just walk away like that?"

I sighed. "That's what I keep asking myself."

And I had yet to come up with an answer that didn't point to something unsavory going down in Nocturne Falls.

I let the topic rest. We had cat food to buy anyway, and in the bright lights of the Shop-n-Save, I wanted to enjoy my domestic errand with Greyson, not worry about what had become of the store's last six employees.

"Tasty Tuna Surprise?" Greyson held up a small can of cat food. "What do you think the surprise is?"

"That it tastes better than it sounds? Throw it in the basket." With his help, I picked out an abundance of cat food, both canned and dry, a bag of chicken-flavored treats, and a jumbo jug of cat litter. Enough to hold Spider in good stead until this thing was all over.

At which point, I guessed I'd be taking him back to the North Pole. Huh. I hadn't considered that until just now, but there was no way I was giving him up. Who would sleep on my hair?

I added a box of chocolate glazed donuts, another six-pack of Dr Pepper, and a cheap spiral-bound notebook to the mix, and we checked out. Greyson eyed the baked goods and the soda, but wisely said nothing. He took the jug of litter and a bag, then I took the remaining two bags and we started the walk back.

"Thanks," I said. "I really appreciate you coming with me on this trip. I'm not really scared to be on my own at night, but you know, strange town and all that. I'm still getting my bearings."

"You don't need to be afraid in Nocturne Falls, but being smart is never a bad move. If you ever need me, just call. I'll be there."

"Very sweet of you. You should probably give me your number then."

He smiled. "And you should give me yours."

"I will this time, promise." I liked him. Maybe more than was prudent. He was a vampire, and I really knew very little about him, but he worked for the town, and after what he'd told me about the Ellinghams, it didn't seem like they'd hire just anybody to represent them. Especially not as one of the characters on the street who interacted with the tourists.

The rest of the walk back was small talk and comfortable silence, both of which I enjoyed. Greyson was easy to be with. I considered telling him who I really was, then decided against it. It was early days yet, and my job was to be here as Lilibeth, so that's what I was sticking to.

For now, anyway.

We reached the entrance to the warehouse and stopped at the door. Main Street was quieter but not nearly deserted. We put our packages on the sidewalk and exchanged numbers then I picked up my bags again and gestured toward his. "Will you hand the rest to me?"

He hesitated. "I know I'm not on the approved list, but I should help you bring these things up."

I smiled. "It's okay. I can handle it. I'm still stronger than the average human, you know."

"It's not about that. It's about being a gentleman."

"Even better. But I got it." I held out my hands. I really didn't want to get on Toly's bad side, even if the payoff was more time with Greyson. Hot guys took a back seat to getting this job done.

He handed me his bag and helped me balance it with the jug of litter. Then he lifted his hands, threaded his fingers through my hair and kissed me.

I lost my breath for a moment, but just as I figured out what he was doing, the kiss was over, leaving me wanting more.

Nicely played, Greyson.

But those words stayed in my head. No immediate verbal response came to me. Outside of *wow*, which didn't seem like an adult response.

He smiled. "See you Saturday, Lilibeth."

I nodded. "Saturday."

Then he drifted into the shadows and was gone. It happened so fast, I almost doubted he'd actually been there, except for the lingering scent of cinnamon.

In a happy sort of daze, I made my way upstairs. The buzz from the wine might be gone, but the buzz from Greyson and his kiss had taken its place very effectively.

I dumped the bags on the kitchen counter, unpacked the goods and put them away, then gave Spider a can of food to see how he'd like it.

As if not liking it was even a possibility. He purred while he ate, and his happy noises added to my general euphoria.

Life was good. So good, I wasn't ready to go to bed yet.

Five minutes later, I was standing in Bertie's old apartment, wobbling slightly from the magical aftershocks of slipping under the crack of his door. As everything balanced, I started looking around, going for the pile of mail that had been on his kitchen counter.

It was gone. So was the calendar next to the fridge.

I checked the bathroom. Toothpaste, toothbrush, razor, all gone. In the bedroom, the walk-in closet was empty. The whole place was as spotless as a hotel room and just as impersonal. It appeared everything that had belonged to Bertie had been stripped away.

The only difference between now and the last time I'd been in here was that the cleaning service had come through.

I didn't know what to think. Had Toly told the cleaning service to get rid of everything? Was this how he handled an employee that went missing? Erase and move on? It was really strange.

With nothing to investigate, I went back to my apartment and got ready for bed. I was definitely calling my father in the morning, but first I needed to make some sense of what I knew.

I got out the files I'd been given and looked through them one more time, studying the pictures. Bertie had cropped navy hair with a sprinkling of gray throughout. He'd been older, probably working at the shop because he'd earned it, and based on the color of his hair, his magic skills had been high. The rest of the employees all seemed to fall into that category as well. But then, you had to be reasonably gifted to work here.

I grunted in disappointment. I'd hoped to see some new detail or something that might spark a thought or make a connection as to why these elves might have left.

But nothing new popped out at me. Six elves

had quit. All of them without any previous complaints or indication that they had been thinking about leaving. At least none that Juniper could tell me about.

I put the files in the nightstand drawer, turned out the light and lay down. I stared at the ceiling in frustration. I was going to have to talk to Toly. I didn't want to, but I needed to hear his take on all this.

I rolled over, trying to get comfortable, but my apprehension about the impending conversation was making me fidgety.

Spider jumped up on the bed, curled into a ball against my stomach and was snoring softly within minutes.

"Must be nice." I petted him, enjoying the silky feel of his coat. "I hope you don't mind the cold when we head north. Maybe we'll get you a sweater."

I shifted again, seeking a position that would lead to sleep. Then I made myself think about Greyson instead of Toly. Not such a hard thing to do. Especially if I replayed that over-too-soon kiss.

Then finally, with a smile on my face, I drifted off.

I woke to someone touching my face. I sat up with a start and nearly tossed Spider off the bed. Okay, not someone exactly. I caught my breath and gave him a stern look. "Spider, you little dickens.

Are you trying to give me a heart attack? No paws to the face this early."

He trilled at me, tail in the air, and lifted his front foot again. Someone wanted breakfast.

The clock read eight thirty.

"Fine, I'm getting up." In sleep pants and a T-shirt, I padded into the kitchen and opened a can of food for him, then refilled his dry food and gave him fresh water while he ate.

The job of cat mothering done, I took my phone off the charger, grabbed a Dr Pepper and the box of donuts, and went to sit on the couch. I turned the TV on. It went right to the Weather Channel. I left it there for background noise. I figured it would be a decent day. It was Georgia in April. How bad could it be?

I sent Juniper a quick text. She'd be headed down to the store soon.

Checked Bertie's last night after all. Cleaned out. We can talk later.

Her response came in three minutes. *Weird. Def talk later. Have fun with Coop. ;)*

Ah, yes. My non-date. I thought about canceling with Cooper, but I wanted to ask him some of the same questions I'd asked Greyson last night to see if I could get any further.

Then it occurred to me that Cooper, as a town employee *and* a firefighter, might have access to that elevator too. There had to be stuff down there that could catch on fire. I grimaced. I was really going to have to be nice to him today. Like, flirty nice. Ugh.

"Oh, Spider, the things this job is making me do." I sighed and shook my head. His never came up from the food bowl.

I needed to talk to my dad, too, but that wasn't happening until I injected some much-needed caffeine and sugar into my system. After the satisfying hiss of my Dr Pepper being opened, I munched a donut and watched the forecast for the day. High sixties. Or full-on summer for a winter elf.

Definitely time to buy some sandals. Which meant I was going to need a pedicure, because my little piggies needed a makeover. Of course, all of that assumed I was going to be here awhile. Was I? No clue. I wasn't getting very far figuring out why the employees had left.

Why hadn't Bertie taken his stuff? I felt like if I could answer that, I'd shed some light on the whole thing.

Which was why a conversation with Toly had to happen.

I finished my donut and half the Dr Pepper then gave the snow globe a good shake. I turned down the volume on the TV while I waited for my dad to appear.

By the start of donut number two, he showed. "Morning, sweetheart."

I wiped chocolate glaze off my mouth with the back of my hand. "Hi, Dad. How's it going up there?"

"Good. Your mother's decided to take up scrapbooking." He made a face. "The dining room table looks like Martha Stewart threw up on it."

My mother and her arts and crafts. "You enjoy that."

He laughed. "Thanks. How's it going for you?"

"Well…I have some questions. And some news. Maybe." I shrugged a little. "I'm not sure where to start, so this may be a little disjointed, but there's definitely more to this whole thing than the former employees being poached away by another company. In fact, I'm pretty sure the elves didn't go missing of their own accord."

"What makes you think that?"

"For one, Bertie's apartment—"

"I meant to talk to you about that. We'd like you to document that his things are still there. If you can, take some pictures, save them to a flash drive then send it to us through the Santa's Bag."

"No can do. What I was going to say was that Bertie's apartment, as of last night, is empty and ready for a new employee."

"Any chance he came back in the middle of the night and did it himself?"

"I doubt it." Mostly because I'd been in there in the middle of the night. "My best guess is the cleaning service that comes every week took care of it. Do you know who they are?"

"Not without having the Financial Department dig into the store's books. We leave those contracts up to the managers at each store. Toly would have all that information."

"Great." I downed some more Dr Pepper. "I need to talk to him, but I'm not looking forward to it. He seems easily upset. And prone to bouts of crankiness."

"Don't make things too hard on yourself. You do have to work for the man a little while longer."

"I know. And I won't." Donut number three called to me. I ignored its chocolatey siren song to carry on the conversation. "Here's a question for you. Did the town of Nocturne Falls contact you about this situation, or did you already know about it? You being you or Uncle Kris."

"We knew about it because of the census, but within a week of that, the Ellinghams reached out to us. Just a weird coincidence. What makes you ask?"

"Curiosity. Sort of a chicken and egg thing. Doesn't matter. One more question. Do you know about the elevator that's in the vestibule of the building here? The one that's for Nocturne Falls employees only?"

He nodded. "Sure do. One of the stipulations of

buying the building was deeding that particular part of the property to the town."

"So…the elevator's not actually owned by the company?"

"Right."

"Huh. Where does it go?"

He laughed. "The sewers and electrical, sweetheart. Why? Having some plumbing issues?"

"No." So much for that. But I could see why the town wouldn't want people down there. You could mess up a town's ability to function pretty badly by damaging either one of those systems. "Just wondering. Toly has kittens anytime someone goes near it."

"That's because we have an understanding with the town that it's off-limits to us and our employees. We incur all costs for damages caused by the actions of our workers, and after three strikes, they can recall our deed."

"No wonder he freaks out about it." I leaned forward. "Could they really take the property back over that elevator?"

"According to the sales contract we signed, yes."

That made me think there could definitely be more down there than sewer and electrical, but if my dad had known what else it was, I was sure he would have told me. "How about that." I sat back and gave in to the urge for another donut.

"By the way, I found an answer to your

questions about breaks and the quota. Believe it or not, Georgia state law doesn't require breaks for workers. As a company, however, we mandate half an hour minimum for lunch and another fifteen-minute break when the shift is eight hours or more."

"Toly's definitely not following that policy. Lunch is twenty minutes, and I did not get a fifteen-minute break when I worked eight hours."

"That's not enough reason for workers to quit, though." He frowned. "Is it?"

"No, I don't think so. Look, don't do anything about that just yet. I don't want him to think I'm making waves at corporate."

"Understood. About the sales quota, there is none. The stores make more than enough money, and really, they're how we see what toys are trending, test new products, find out what kids want next, that sort of thing. We aren't so concerned with sales that we demand figures be met."

"Huh. Then Toly's using the idea of the quota to keep his employees busy."

"Could be. You have plans for the day?"

"Yep. Doing a little town research, then working the evening shift. Five to close, which is ten o'clock. And I may try to talk to Toly. I'll have to see how brave I feel."

He laughed. "All right. Have a good one."

"You too. Tell Mom I said hi."

"Will do."

The snow settled. I put the globe back, kicked my feet up onto the coffee table and concentrated on the donut while my mind whirled around the problem at hand.

What on earth was going on? So many things seemed to be more than what they were.

Spider came over and crawled into my lap. One thing I knew for sure. No one in their right mind would purposefully leave this sweet animal behind.

Which meant whatever had happened to Bertie had happened against his will. Or had at least resulted in him being unable to return. What could that be?

A chill shook me.

Was Bertie dead?

I knew right then I had to find a way to talk to the police and see if any John Does had shown up lately. But that wasn't going to be easy. As far as they knew, I had just moved here. What authority did I have to be asking about missing-persons reports and unclaimed bodies? And if the Ellinghams were as on top of what was happening in this town as Greyson said, would they even allow the police to release that kind of info?

It had to be logged somewhere, right? Just because they were vampires and this town was full of supernaturals didn't mean crime didn't happen or get reported. No one was above the law.

Maybe Cooper could help. As a firefighter, he had to know people. At the very least he could point me in the right direction.

And I had to do all that without Toly getting a whiff.

I scratched Spider's belly. "Today is going to be very interesting."

With a sigh, I reached for a fourth donut. Something told me it was going to be that kind of day. And not just because I had to be extra nice to Cooper.

9

I was so distracted by the thoughts in my head that I almost went down to meet Cooper without my purse. At the last second, I threw the strap over my shoulder, double-checked that I had my phone and locked up.

I was three minutes early.

Of course, he was already there. Hands in his pockets, he greeted me with a grin. For a moment, I was standing outside my dorm hall. I shook off the memory as he spoke. "Nice day, huh?"

"Sure is. Blue sky, sun is shining—"

"And I have a pretty girl to keep me company."

I smiled. So sue me. "Thanks." I chewed on my lip. I needed to say something back. "You look nice." He did. Jeans and T-shirt on some guys could look schlumpy, but on Cooper, they highlighted his casual good looks and exceptional physique.

"Thanks. You look nice, too."

I'd warred between looking cute enough to encourage his attention and not so cute that he thought I was into him. Considering I needed his help, I'd leaned toward more cute rather than less cute. But I was still just in jeans, a floaty top and a cardigan. Nothing fancy. Although I'd gone with ballet flats instead of boots. It just wasn't boot weather. "Where are we off to today?"

"First a tour of the town, then a stop for something sweet—or several somethings sweet—then a different way home to see some more of the town."

"Sounds good. Lead the way." As we walked toward Main, I hoped there would be plenty of openings for me to ask the questions I needed to. Seeing the town was great, and might give me more insight into the whole situation, but my head ached with the amount of unanswered questions I had.

There wasn't much chance for small talk initially. Cooper took the tour-guide role seriously, pointing out all sorts of things along the way, telling me about the shops and the shop owners, including a jewelry store owned by a fae woman who'd apparently given up the crown of her kingdom for the love of a gargoyle.

"She really walked away from becoming queen in the name of love?"

Cooper looked pleased to have shared such a story with me. "Sure did."

"Wow."

His brows lifted. "You seem shocked. Wouldn't you do the same?"

His question threw me for a second, and I had to remind myself he didn't know who I really was. "Of course I would."

He made a face. "Some women wouldn't. I know that."

Maybe I was being paranoid, but that sounded like it was aimed at me. The real me. "What makes you say that?"

He shook his head. "It's nothing. Something that happened a long time ago."

"But you were obviously affected by it. Or her."

He frowned, and a few moments of silence passed between us. "I was in love with someone once. But we didn't work out because of the choices she made. Choices based on what her family might think about me."

"That's not—" I was about to say *what happened*. Then I caught myself. "Right. Just not right."

"No, it wasn't."

Clearly we had different memories of what actually gone down. But this was neither the time nor the place to remind him that he was the one who'd flaked on me right before Christmas break, refusing to come north with me and meet my parents.

And that he'd been the one who'd broken things off. He'd been the one who'd decided he couldn't handle being involved with a *princess*. I scowled, unable to forget the way he'd said that word to me, calling me that like it was my fault for being next in line for the winter throne.

As if I had any say in who my family was.

"Hey, you all right?"

I glanced over at him and his stupid handsome face. "What?"

"You look like you ate a bad fig."

"Oh, no, I was just..." Think fast. And lose the attitude. "Remembering I have to work tonight."

He laughed. "I thought working at the shop was a big deal. That you had to be on a waiting list to even get the job."

"It is. And you do. But Toly's kind of..." I glanced around like I was hoping no one could overhear us. "Mean."

Coop nodded. "Yeah, I've heard from the other workers he can be tough sometimes."

"I get it, he's the manager and the responsibilities are all on his shoulders, but I didn't expect him to be such a task master, you know?"

Cooper mulled that over. "You'll probably end up leaving too, then."

"What do you mean?" This could be the opening I was looking for.

He shrugged. "People don't stay at that store.

Sure, some do. Juniper and Buttercup have been there awhile."

"And Owen?"

"I don't know him very well. He doesn't come out much. Actually, I don't think he's ever come out after work with us."

"Yeah, he strikes me as pretty serious. I bet Toly loves him."

We both snickered, and before I could ask another question, Cooper pointed to the park ahead of us. "We're going to detour through there." He leaned in. "The gargoyles that work the fountain are real gargoyles, but the tourists think they're animatronic."

"Cool." And it was. But I wasn't ready to drop the original subject. "Hey, did you know any of the employees that left?"

We crossed the street at the light. "Not the last one, but the one before him, Nora, I knew her. Nice lady. A little older, but she loved to hang out with us at Howler's. She made me cookies on my birthday."

"That was sweet."

He smiled, his eyes filled with the memory. "Yeah. I can't believe she left without saying goodbye."

"I take it that seems unlike her?"

"Very much."

"Did you have any idea she was thinking about quitting?"

"Not a clue."

It was a pattern then. If two could be considered a pattern. They might have been leaving Toly notes, but they weren't telling anyone else they were quitting. Or why.

We made our way around to the front of the fountain. Tourists were gathered in a semi-circle around the gargoyle. He was talking to them and making jokes and spraying water at them unexpectedly. It was a riot. And very clever.

We watched for a while, not saying anything, just taking in the show. I surreptitiously studied Cooper. The years had been kind to him. Sure, we were elves and time was generally kind to all of us, but we did age.

Cooper looked better now than he had in college. More sure of himself. Less lost puppy, more alpha dog. And he wasn't nearly as cocky as he had been in those days, although to be honest, I'd been attracted to that kind of blatant confidence back then. Still was to some extent.

It took a man with a solid sense of who he was to date the Winter King's daughter. Cooper just hadn't had enough of that sense back then to stay.

In light of our ages and the bad decisions most people make during their youth, I should have forgiven him a long time ago. But he'd broken my heart.

More than that, he'd taught me that I was

always going to be judged because of the family I came from and my position in that family.

That had hurt worse. Because there wasn't a damn thing I could do about that.

He looked over. "What?"

I shifted my gaze back to the fountain for a moment. "Nothing." I met his eyes again. "I could eat, though."

He grinned. "You're gonna love the next place. C'mon."

We crossed the street again, back to Main, then up a few more blocks until we turned down Black Cat Boulevard. The smell of sugar and coffee hit me the second we rounded the corner.

"I like it already."

He laughed. "You have no idea."

"Is that the place?" I pointed to the storefront bearing the name The Hallowed Bean. I wasn't a huge coffee drinker. Dr Pepper was definitely my beverage of choice, but I wouldn't turn down a cup of java either. Especially if it was a mocha or a caramel latte.

"Nope. But that place is really good too." He stopped and pulled open a door. "Here we are."

The wave of chocolatey, sugary goodness that washed over me almost took my breath. I stood for a moment inhaling. It was transcendent.

Cooper nudged me. "Don't pass out now, there's more to come."

I stepped inside with him right behind me. The shop was so thick with delicious smells I swear I already tasted chocolate on my tongue. "Is this heaven?"

He grinned. "No, this is Delaney's Delectables."

The shop was bustling and I could see why. A horseshoe of glass display cases showed off trays of truffles and other chocolates, cakes, cookies, cupcakes, candied apples, and confections I didn't even know the name of.

"I should have gotten a job here."

"Pretty sure hiring a winter elf would end up costing them money. What do you want to try?"

I looked at him. "Are you kidding? All of it."

We got in line. Two attractive women hustled behind the counter, filling orders. Both of them—one tall with straight dark hair and a vine tattoo on one arm, the other shorter with wavy brunette hair—were definitely supernaturals. What kind, obviously, I had no idea.

I leaned in toward Cooper. "What are they?" I whispered.

"Taller one is a werewolf, shorter one is a vampire," he whispered back. "Ivy, the werewolf, is the wife of my chief's brother. The vampire is Delaney. She owns the shop."

"How is she here? It's daylight. I thought vampires couldn't be out in the sun."

He shrugged. "They can't, but she's an

125

Ellingham. They have some family secret that makes them immune."

I nodded, more interested to taste the goods than ever.

When it was our turn to order, I let Cooper go first because I wasn't ready. Ivy greeted him like an old friend.

His selections fit in a small box. Mine...didn't. Ivy handed me a full-size shopping bag. Hey, I wasn't eating it all here. Although I did wonder if that particular charge to the credit card was one my father would question.

Well, you know what? He was just going to have to suck it up. There was no way I was leaving any of this behind.

Cooper's brows rose as he looked at my haul. "You know you can come back, right?"

"I know. I got some for Juniper." Well, I'd been planning to share, but now I was definitely giving her some.

His amusement didn't fade. "You want to find a spot to eat some of this stuff?"

"This will probably seem odd coming from me, but we should have some actual food first. Is that okay? When do you have to be back to the firehouse?"

"Not until tonight. And yes, let's get some lunch. How's pizza sound?"

"Perfect. I can't work my shift tonight on sugar

alone. I need some healthy veggies to balance things out."

He gave me an odd look. "So are you going to get a salad?"

"No, I meant the tomato sauce."

He snorted. "All right. We're off to Salvatore's for some health food then."

I love pizza, who doesn't? But I was really hoping that sitting down to a meal would give me a chance to get back to my questions about the employees and how I might find out if the police had any reports.

I could stop by the police station on my own, but what were the odds of that working? No, right now, Cooper was my best bet.

Half an hour later, we were squared away at a table for two and a piping-hot Salvatore's king pie, their version of a supreme, was sitting in front of us in all its gooey, cheesy glory. Really, it was a work of art. My mouth watered in anticipation.

"See?" I said. "Look at all those healthy veggies."

Cooper peered at the pizza. "Yes, somewhere under the sausage and pepperoni I see peppers, onions and mushrooms."

"All healthy." I slid a slice onto my plate to let it cool as he did the same. "You eat here a lot?"

"They deliver. We get pizza from them all the time at the station."

"I should take a menu with me then."

"Definitely. Their subs aren't bad either." He lifted his slice, folded it in half and took a bite. He made a happy noise that sort of startled me. Let's just say food wasn't the only reason he made that sound. And I knew firsthand what that other reason was.

I ate some of my pizza too and understood immediately why that sound had come out of him. "Oh, this is the stuff."

Cooper nodded. "Told ya," he said around a mouthful.

We ate for a bit, taking the edge off. Then I started in. "So I've been thinking…"

"About?"

"Those employees. Do you think something bad happened to them?"

He wiped his mouth with a napkin. "Such as?"

"I don't know. But it's weird that they'd leave so abruptly. Especially since working at a Santa's Workshop is such a primo job."

He nodded slowly, like he was thinking. "I agree with that. But I don't know. I feel like I would have heard something if that was the case."

"Why would you have heard? Because you're in the fire department?"

"Sort of." He took a second slice. "My chief is Titus Merrow, and his brother is the sheriff in town. He's the one who's married to Ivy. Anyway, we tend to know if something's going on. Not always, but a lot of the time."

I felt like I'd just hit the jackpot. Time to get flirty. I smiled, hoping there was nothing stuck in my teeth. "Do you think you could ask your chief if he's heard of anything? Like a John Doe or a missing-persons report that's been filed?"

Cooper frowned. "You think it's that sort of situation? That one of them might actually be dead?"

"I really have no idea. But I deserve to know what's going on at the place I work. I don't want to be next."

His expression softened. "I don't want that either." He rested his arm on the table. "I'll ask around. See what I can find out."

I smiled a little bigger. "Thank you. That means a lot to me."

He returned my grin. "Enough to be my date at the fund-raiser tomorrow night?"

"The thing you were making up those baskets for?" I dug into my second piece.

"Yep. It's nothing fancy. It's at the firehouse. It's a spaghetti dinner."

"Sure. I'd love to. I've never been in a firehouse before." And if it was a fund-raiser at the firehouse, that meant the chief would probably be there. And so might his brother, the sheriff. I had to go. "Is there really a pole you slide down?"

He laughed. "Sure is. You want to go down it?"

I stared at him. "Um, *yes*."

He smirked. "I can make that happen."

"I'll remember not to wear a dress."

And just like that, I was going on a second date with Cooper. Well, Lilibeth was going on a second date. But let's be honest. This *was* a date, no matter how you sliced it. Oh boy. This was not how I'd pictured any of this turning out.

We walked back through town on Broomstick Lane, a street that ran parallel to Main. It was two blocks away from the main drag and a bit quieter, but still had a lot of cute little shops. I made note of a boutique where I might be able to get a pair of sandals.

We came to a small park, nothing like the one with the fountain and the gargoyles, just a pretty block of grass and old shade trees with some benches and paved pathways radiating out from a statue of a woman in an old-timey dress.

The second bench we came to was unoccupied, so we sat. I put my shopping bag down and picked out the box on top. I had no idea what was in it, but that wasn't going to stop me.

Cooper opened his box of sweets too. "I was going to share these with you."

I looked at his scant offerings. A couple of truffles, two cookies and a piece of chocolate bark. "I feel bad taking any of that. There's so little in there."

He laughed. "Summer elves don't have the same sweet cravings that winter elves do."

I opened my box and found it was filled with truffles. Score. I selected one and took a bite. Raspberry. Double score. "I know. Summer elves like fruit." The chocolate melted over my tongue and addled my brain with its deliciousness. "You like peaches."

He stared at me. "How do you know that?"

I stopped mid-bite. *Snowballs*. Lilibeth wasn't supposed to know that. I shrugged and tried to play it off. "Am I right? I figured since you live in Georgia and that's what this state is known for..."

"Good guess. I do like peaches. And they are pretty incredible here." But he was still looking at me like I shouldn't have known that.

"Plus"—I pointed the remains of my truffle at him—"you mentioned something at Howler's about the cobbler being the only dessert worth eating. I put two and two together."

Way to think fast, brain.

"Oh, yeah." He nodded and I knew then I was safe. "That cobbler is amazing."

We sat for a while, me eating more truffles than I should and neither of us talking much. It was nice.

I studied the statue. I couldn't read the plaque from here, but the woman on the stand had to be some kind of historical figure important to the town. I was about to ask Cooper, when I noticed a woman jogging through the other side of the park.

She looked really familiar, but I couldn't place her. I leaned in toward Cooper. "Any chance you know who that woman is over there? The one jogging in the bright blue sneakers?"

He looked, then shook his head. "No. Why?"

"I feel like I should know her, but I have no idea why. And really, how could I know her? I just moved here." Unless she had gone to the same college as Cooper and I, but she seemed ten years older than we were.

"She's probably been in the store. Maybe you waited on her."

"Yeah, that's probably it." Except it didn't feel like that's where I knew her from. I kept my eyes on her long enough to make out that she wasn't wearing an elf bracelet but as she disappeared from view, nothing else came to me.

I packed up my sweets. "I should get back. I have to work in a couple hours."

"Okay, we're not far."

We headed back down Broomstick Lane on the way to my building with Cooper pointing out more sites on the way. Thanks to his tour, I was actually starting to get the layout of the town.

At the door, I turned to say goodbye. "I'd ask

you up, but there's this rule about guests having to be approved and—"

"I'm already on the list. I hang out with Juniper and Buttercup all the time. But no worries. I didn't expect an invite. Just promise me you won't eat the rest of those sweets at once."

"I won't. Probably." He laughed. "I had a really great day. Thanks for taking the time to show me around."

"My pleasure. Thanks for agreeing to come to the fund-raiser with me."

"Don't forget I get to slide down the pole."

He snorted. "I won't."

"Good. I'll see you Friday night. Should I just come to the firehouse?"

Cooper nodded. "It starts at six, but you can get there before then. Especially if you want to go down the pole without too much of an audience. I'll text you directions. I'm working that day or I'd come pick you up."

"I don't mind." We traded phone numbers. "Hey, can I bring Juniper or Buttercup if they're not working?"

"Sure, the more the merrier."

Plus, it would be less like a date that way. "Okay, great. See you." For some reason, I leaned in and kissed him on the cheek. Maybe I felt bad for basically lying to him and knowing that he'd never have bothered giving me a tour or any of this if he'd known who I really was. Or maybe I wanted him to know I really did appreciate him spending his time on me.

Either way, he turned as I leaned in and our mouths met.

I jerked back. "Sorry, I didn't mean—well, I did mean to, but not on the lips."

His smile was slow and weighty. "Don't be sorry. I'm not." Then the smile flattened. "But I'm really not looking for a relationship. Especially not with a winter elf." He shoved a hand through his gorgeous hair. "I'm not judging you—"

"Sounds that way, but don't worry about it. I'm not looking for a relationship either."

His gaze steeled, and I thought he was going to snap back at me. "You're right. I shouldn't judge you by what happened in my past."

He sighed and looked down the street, then shook his head. "You'd think after all these years I'd be over her."

My heart clenched in a mix of pain and regret. I really didn't want to hear this. Not from the man who'd been the source of my pain for so long. "Just friends is cool, right?"

He glanced back at me, but his gaze was distant, lost in memory. "Just friends."

I backed toward the door, mumbled, "See you Friday," and went in.

I was shaking a little as I unlocked my door and

went inside. That was not at all how I'd imagined the day going. I could still feel his mouth on mine, even though the contact had only lasted half a second.

It had been enough to remind me of our time together. I put my shopping bag down and leaned against the kitchen counter, chilled by the thought that it could have done the same thing for him. Would it be enough to make him realize who I really was?

No. That was silly. A half-second accidental kiss wasn't enough to do anything.

Except here I was, trembling like an idiot.

I took a breath. Well, the kiss had served one purpose. I was finally looking forward to going to work.

I ended up twenty minutes early, but better to look eager, right? I fiddled with my apron to buy time behind the counter with Juniper. "How's the day been?"

"Busy. Same as always." Then she nudged me and made moony eyes at me. "So? How was it?"

"What?" I knew what she meant, but it was more fun to make her work for it.

"Your date with Cooper."

"It wasn't a date." It was totally a date.

She exhaled a hard breath. "Fine. Your *outing*."

"It was nice." I decided to stop tormenting her and pulled on the apron strings while I gave her the rundown. "We walked around town, went to see the fountain, bought a ton of delicious things at this shop called Delaney's Delectables, had maybe the best pizza I've ever had at Salvatore's, did a little more walking around, sat in the park for a bit and came home." The kiss was staying in the vault.

"Delaney's? And Salvatore's? Wow, he was looking to impress."

"No, he wasn't. I bought my own stuff at Delaney's." Although he had bought lunch. "He was just showing me around."

"Yeah, okay. You keep telling yourself that."

"Hey, are you working tomorrow night?"

"No, I'm on day shift. We both are."

"Excellent." I tied my apron. "You want to go to the spaghetti dinner at the fire hall with me? It's a fund-raiser for the school. And Cooper invited me."

She went up on her tiptoes. "Um, *yes*." Then she hesitated. "Did you ask if we could slide down the pole?"

I held my hand up for a high five. "Already taken care of."

She slapped her palm against mine. "Nicely done."

"Also..." I reached into my purse and took out the wax paper bag I'd made up for her. It had an assortment of the things I'd gotten at Delaney's. "These are for you. From Delaney's."

"Thanks!" Her eyes widened as she looked inside. "Ooo, dinner is served."

We both laughed as Buttercup rolled up to the counter as chill as ever. "Hey."

"Hey," we both said back to her.

I handed her an apron. "Here you go."

"Thanks." She pulled it over her head. "Guess it's you and me, tonight, Lilibeth."

"Yep. Unfortunately for you, I'm probably still going to need help with stuff. This is only my second shift."

Buttercup nodded. "No worries. We got this." She looked around. "Where's Owen?"

Juniper jerked her thumb toward the warehouse. "Toly called him into his office for a *talk*."

"That's not good." Buttercup stared at the shop's back door.

"Are the talks with Toly always bad?" I remembered what Juniper had told me, but I wondered what Buttercup thought.

She frowned and shook her head. Her spikey black hair didn't move. "Pretty much. Not always, sure, but nine times out of ten, if you're in there, you're in trouble."

Just then the warehouse door swung open and Toly came through. He headed straight for us. "Juniper, we'll see you in the morning. Buttercup, you're on the register as needed and also as backup for Lilibeth. Lilibeth, the dolls section needs straightening, then there's a new shipment of building blocks to be inventoried and stocked. If you need me for anything, call. I'm off to my granddaughter's for dinner in a little bit."

No one moved.

He clapped his hands. "Off to work, ladies, off to work. Juniper, don't keep them from their jobs. They're on the clock."

Juniper gave me a look, then waved and headed for the warehouse. Buttercup started straightening a display by the front door.

I didn't go anywhere, just shifted my gaze to look down at Toly. He might intimidate them, but not me. Of course, my circumstances for being here were very different. "Where's Owen?"

Toly pushed his glasses back on his nose. "He worked this morning. He's off now."

I glanced back at the warehouse before meeting Toly's gaze again. "I thought I'd see him." And was starting to worry that I hadn't. I smiled. "Just trying to get to know my fellow employees."

Toly smiled too, but it seemed strained. "Very commendable, very commendable, but there will be time. It's only your second day. All right, now. Have a good night. I'm off to dinner." He scampered away like he was afraid I'd ask more questions.

Which I would have.

Buttercup sidled up next to me. "He's a little squirrely, that one. All those years at the Factory must have taken their toll on him."

"I don't think that's it. But I agree that he's squirrely. He could be a little less...bossy."

"Well, he is the boss."

"Still." At least with him gone, I'd have no opportunity to have that talk with him. Yes, I needed to do it, but needing to and wanting to were two very different things.

Getting the dolls straightened and reorganized took a solid hour, but I helped two little girls pick out just the right one while I was over there, which wasn't as horrendous as I'd thought dealing with kids would be. They were cute and polite and pretty awesome. After that, I headed to the warehouse to get the new blocks that needed to be inventoried. I gave Buttercup a wave on my way.

She returned it with a nod, her hands occupied with bagging merchandise. She'd been steady at the register most of the night. It was pretty busy with customers, more than I'd thought for a Thursday, but I realized in a town like Nocturne Falls weeknights probably weren't too much different than weekends because of the influx of tourists.

No wonder this place turned over so much merchandise. I could see why my dad and Uncle Kris didn't want to close this location.

It gave me a renewed sense of determination. I would figure this out and get this site back on track. And in doing so, I might find a real place for myself in this company. I could be a problem solver. That had a nice sound to it. And it felt purposeful, which was even better.

Maybe this was what I was meant to do.

I walked back through the rows of stock until I came to the aisle specifically for new arrivals. I wheeled a dolly cart into place and started loading it when I heard the apartment elevator chime. Maybe it was Juniper. I peered around the end cap to see Owen getting out. Despite his dress shirt and tie, he looked melancholy. The same as he had the first time I'd met him. Maybe that was just his face. Or he was bummed that wherever he was going required a tie.

That seemed plausible.

I stepped into the aisle and caught a whiff of his piney, musky aftershave. It smelled like something his dad had probably worn and Owen had never bothered to see if there was anything better. Poor guy. He was such an odd duck. "Hey, Owen. You okay?"

He glanced up, his eyebrows lifting ever so slightly, then they fell as his eyes narrowed. "Lilibeth, right?"

I nodded. Was my name that hard to remember? "Yes, I'm fine, thank you."

"I, uh, just wondered since Juniper said you got called into Toly's office. I hear that's not always a good thing."

"Oh, yes. No, it was fine. He just wanted to make sure I could handle the Snowy Saturday shimmer if he couldn't be here."

"Is he going somewhere?"

Owen shrugged. "He didn't say." Then he checked his watch. "Sorry, I have to go. I'm off to dinner."

That would explain the tie. And the aftershave. Must be a date. I held my hands up. "Don't let me stop you. Have fun."

"Thanks." He shuffled off, leaving me alone in the warehouse.

I realized then he hadn't said he was meeting someone, just off to dinner. Alone? Nothing wrong with that, but then why the rush? Odd guy, but nice enough.

I went back to work and a new question presented itself. Why would Toly need to make sure Owen could handle the shimmer? First of all, it was part of Toly's job as store manager. Secondly, we were all pretty capable magic-wise.

Another new thought occurred to me. Was Toly losing his magic? I'd never heard of that happening, but anything was possible. And if he was, could that be somehow related to the employees leaving?

But I couldn't find a bridge between those two things. Not even a rickety one.

I sighed and the sound was oddly loud in the deep quiet of the warehouse, reminding me I was alone. And Toly was at dinner at his granddaughter's. I stepped out of the aisle and glanced at his office. The pebbled glass in the door was dark. I walked over, nerves prickling my skin, and tried the handle.

Locked, as I knew it would be. Of course, locked doors weren't much of a barrier for me. But did I want to risk it? What if Buttercup came looking for me? Or Toly hadn't actually left for his granddaughter's yet?

I decided to come back later that night, after the shop was closed and everyone was asleep. Then I'd slip in and do a little digging. Maybe I could find out the name of the cleaning service without ever having to talk to Toly. That would be worth it.

I finished loading the dolly, hauled it back to the store and got to work stocking the shelves with the new stuff. The rest of the night went by pretty fast. Buttercup's dry sense of humor and snarkiness were on point. I liked her a lot. She reminded me a bit of Lark.

Which reminded me I hadn't talked to my friend in forever. And that made me a little sad. I'm sure she was busy with her jet-setting friends.

At least I was making some new ones. Whether or not they'd stick around after they found out who I really was remained to be seen. Although, did it matter? I'd be working whatever new job I was assigned to at the North Pole and they'd...still be here, I guess. While I'd be back to having no real friends.

The whole thing made me feel a little down,

which wasn't like me at all. What I really wanted to do was go upstairs, snuggle with Spider and stuff myself full of Delaney's Delectables.

Instead, I trudged up to the check-out counter with an unmarked Sister Sarah doll and started digging for the pricing gun.

"Half an hour," Buttercup whispered.

"Until what?" I asked, thinking something really cool was about to happen.

"Until we're out of here."

Gun in hand, I stood up. Cool enough for me. "It's nine thirty already?"

She nodded, grinning for the first time all evening. "Yep. You up for drinks at Howler's?"

I groaned with genuine disappointment. "I would love to hang out with you, but I have to work the day shift tomorrow." By which I meant sneak into Toly's office and do some digging. But her offer picked me up a bit. "And I'm going to that fund-raiser thing at the fire hall tomorrow night. Otherwise, I would so be taking you up on the drinks offer."

She wiggled her dark brows. "The firehouse fund-raiser, huh? Are you going to that because of a certain elven firefighter?"

I laughed softly. "Yes. He asked me."

"Be warned. He's not looking for anything serious. I mean, he dates a lot, for sure, but those dates never turn into anything."

"He told me he wasn't interested in a relationship. Just being friends. I'm completely cool with that."

"Good." She clucked her tongue. "Some chick did a number on him in the past, I can tell you that much."

"Really?" I leaned against the counter. "What have you heard?" This ought to be good. I knew what kind of things Cooper had said about me before.

She shrugged. "Just that he was crazy about her, but she came from one of the major NP families, lots of money, you know, and she ditched him because she was afraid her parents wouldn't approve of her bringing home a summer elf."

Was that what he was telling people? At least he wasn't being too specific. There were a lot of wealthy families in the North Pole, but if he'd said royalty, that would have narrowed it down pretty quickly. "There are two sides to every story, you know."

"I'm sure, but I don't know, for a guy like Cooper? I could get a little May-December thing happening. Even if my parents didn't approve."

I needed to change the subject before I said something I shouldn't. "You know humans use that expression to mean an older man with a younger woman."

"So I've heard, but to us it will always mean a summer elf and a winter elf."

"True." I walked around to the front of the counter, more than ready to be out of here. "This is my first closing shift. What needs to be done?"

Buttercup pulled out a clipboard from under the counter. "Here's the list Toly likes us to follow."

I scanned it quickly and picked out what I thought would be the least desirable jobs. "I'll start with cleaning the bathrooms, then I'll sweep."

She made an incredulous face. "Really?"

"I'm low elf on the totem pole, right? I'll do the dirty work. Literally."

"I'm not going to argue. The cleaning stuff for the bathrooms and the push broom are in the supply closet."

"I'm on it."

Between us, we had the place tidied up and locked tight by ten thirteen. We rode the elevator up together and went off to our separate apartments.

Spider was happy to see me. Or maybe to see his dinner. I was hoping it was both. I fed him, then since there was no Greyson hanging out like a teenage dream in my window, I fixed a frozen dinner and sat in front of the TV for a while, passing the time until I thought it was safe to head back down.

Sitting turned into slouching, which turned into full-on horizontal lying, and I ended up snoozing a little. It worked out. I woke up a couple minutes after one a.m. with Spider curled up on my stomach. An infomercial prattled on about some revolutionary at-home fitness contraption that looked pretty much like a chair.

Not that I'm a fitness contraption expert.

I yawned and eased Spider to the couch, then pushed to a sitting position while doing my best not to disturb him. Because, you know, he had that big presentation to give at the office in the morning and everything.

I got a Dr Pepper and finished off box number two from Delaney's. Man, that stuff was good. I wondered if she could ship to the North Pole. Maybe we could work out a monthly order to be sent through the Santa's Bag.

Worth looking into.

Sugared up and awake, I put on black leggings, a black hoodie with a nice big pouch pocket in the front, and my black lug-soled boots. They were the quietest I had. I looked very burglar-esque. Seemed right.

Out in the hall, I pocketed my keys and my phone, then put my ear to Juniper's and Buttercup's doors. Nothing. I hoped that meant they were deep in sleep. Unless I wanted to take the fire escape, I had no choice but to call the elevator.

But there had to be stairs, right? Wasn't that a

fire code thing? Toly hadn't pointed them out, but by law there had to be some somewhere.

I found a door marked Emergency on the other side of the elevator foyer. I turned on the flashlight on my phone and shone it through the small safety glass window. Yep. Stairs. But I was hesitant to open the door. What if it was one of those doors that locked behind you and the rest of the doors were locked too? What if an alarm went off?

The locked door wasn't such a big deal, but I did not want to explain my way out of an alarm. And having to use my ability to slip under a door twice like that would mean more recovery time at the bottom. Then there was the possibility that the resulting dizziness at the top might make me fall.

Frost it. I was using the elevator. If anyone said anything, I'd tell them I'd left my phone in the store. That would have to do.

I pressed the down button and waited for what felt like three years. When the chime went off with the car's arrival, I swore the sound blasted as loud as an air horn.

I ducked in and hit the button, urging the doors to close as quietly as possible. They didn't, but I didn't hear Juniper or Buttercup opening their apartment doors to see what was going on, either. Even so, my heart was racing. I was not cut out for criminal behavior.

Half a minute later, I stood in the warehouse.

For a couple seconds, that's all I did. I needed to make sure I was completely alone, and as I waited there in the dim space, I knew I was. The whole breaking-and-entering thing was giving me hives.

Sure, I'd done it at Bertie's, but Bertie was out of the picture. Toly could show up at any moment. And if that happened, I guess I'd…I wasn't sure what I'd do actually.

I hoped I didn't have to find out.

The small bit of street light filtering in through the warehouse door transom and the handful of security lights in the warehouse itself gave off just enough illumination to see by, at least with elf eyes. So by the time I was sure no one had followed me down, my eyes were pretty well adjusted. I walked over to Toly's office and tried the door. Still locked.

I did the Saint Nick slide and went under. Inside, I leaned against the door while I waited for everything to stop spinning. Without the benefit of the security lights, the office was almost pitch black. I could see much better out of the pebbled glass window than I could on my side of the door.

My phone was my only option. Using the flashlight was taking a risk, but what was the point of doing this if I didn't get to look around?

I moved right with the hopes of getting away from the glass in the door and knocked into something metal. I winced. Probably a filing cabinet, judging by the unfortunate clanging sound.

The upside was I didn't knock anything over. The downside was that was going to leave a mark. With my knee throbbing, I inched around the filing cabinet and lit my phone up.

I squinted at the brightness of the screen and knew I could forgo the flashlight. This was enough. I grabbed the handle of the top drawer and pulled.

Locked. I tried the one beneath it. Also locked. Turned out, the whole filing cabinet was locked. Oh joy.

But only the top drawer had a lock, which meant once opened, all the drawers would be accessible. So that was good.

What was also good was that I hadn't actually lied to Juniper when I said I could pick locks. I could. Simple ones. You needed a safe cracked, I was *not* your girl. Unless you wanted the whole thing frozen solid and shattered. That I could do. But a little lock like this? Cake. It was a skill I'd taught myself early. Like around fifth grade. What can I say? Once a snooper, always a snooper.

But there was no way I could do what I needed to and hold the phone, but light was kind of imperative if the lock picking was going to happen.

With no other options, I yanked my hoodie off and stuck the phone lengthwise into the front of my bra, right across my cleavage. Made for a better phone holder than anticipated. Nicely done, boobs.

Hands free, I drew on the magic in me and spun

two narrow slivers of ice from my fingertips. I regulated my body temp down to about freezing so the ice wouldn't melt as fast. Normal ice would snap if you tried to use it to pick a lock, but this was magical elven ice. The stuff was like steel. Until it wasn't. Which meant I still had to work fast.

Using the light from my phone, I slipped the picks into the lock and manipulated the tumblers. A filing cabinet lock was about a two on the difficulty scale and took all of six seconds to unlatch.

I dropped the picks. Without contact with me, they'd turn into normal ice and melt, leaving no trace of what I'd just done so long as the wet spot dried before anyone noticed it. I reclaimed my phone, pulled my hoodie back on and began flipping through the files in the first drawer.

Nothing all that interesting. Inventory sheets. Years and years and *years* of inventory sheets. Snooze.

Drawer two got better. Personnel files. I'd come back to that one if I had time.

Drawer three was the one I was looking for. Bills. There was a folder for Georgia Power and Light, one for the town of Nocturne Falls, a handyman service, an electrician, heating and air company, etc., etc.

Then I came to a file marked Thrifty Maids. I opened it and brought my phone closer to the first sheet of paper. There was no owner's name on the bill, just the company and the address and the write-up for a month's worth of weekly cleanings. I fired up my camera and snapped a picture.

The flash blinded me, which I deserved for being so dumb. *Snowballs*. That must have looked like fireworks going off from the other side of the window. I blinked away the glowing fuchsia orb left by the flash, hoping my activities were still undetected.

By the time my sight returned, no one had burst into the office and accosted me, so I assumed I was still in the clear. I went back to snooping, this time in the personnel files.

This drawer was divided into two sections. The six files in the back of the drawer all had a little black dot next to each employee's name. The employee names on the front files had no dots. No college degree required to figure out what that meant.

As much as I wanted to look at my own file, I dug deeper and pulled Bertie's instead. The very first piece of paper in the folder was the note of resignation that he'd written. Very to the point. Probably not fifty words. I thought about taking a picture of it, but after how the last one went, decided against it. Besides, I had copies in the file my dad had given me.

Next was Nora's. Same thing, her letter was first in the sheaf of paperwork. This one was a little longer, but not much. The handwriting was more flowery, too. Full of swirls and loops. But a little shaky, too, like a grandmother's might be.

The third file I pulled belonged to a guy named Will. I remembered him from the dossier because he'd won the skiing gold in the North Pole Games three years running before being transferred here. He'd been the second to leave, after a young woman named Trina, and long before anyone had begun to think it odd. His letter was much longer, but also up front.

This wasn't getting me anywhere. Maybe there'd be something in Toly's desk drawers. I shifted my phone around to get a peek at the rest of the office. It looked exactly the way you'd think a tinker's office would. Stuff everywhere. Stacks of papers on the desk, shelves crammed with books and toy prototypes. Drawings tacked to the wall. From the looks of it, he was still inventing. Good for him, but I was never going to get through this mess in a timely fashion.

I decided to try the desk anyway in hopes of turning up something that would make this clandestine visit worthwhile.

Then the elevator chimed.

I froze for a split second, then turned my phone off and went to the door to find out if I was about to get busted.

I stood to the side and stuck my head around just enough to see through the window. Light appeared from the opening elevator doors. I jerked back. Then took another look to see if I needed to find a hiding place.

That's when I realized the light was coming from the restricted elevator, not the one that went to the apartments. I could just make out a dark shape stepping into the vestibule. They'd be gone in seconds.

Curiosity got the best of me. Without another thought, I magically slipped back under the door. The speed only added to the after effects, causing me to wobble toward the elevator. I felt like I was wading through molasses while being tilted forty-five degrees. Fun. The street door was swinging shut. Or maybe that was a trick of my vision. No, whoever had come out of the elevator had left the building.

I finally reached the vestibule, pushed through that door and nudged the street door open a crack. The dark form I'd seen disappeared around the corner and was gone.

My only lasting impression was that the dark form had also been tall and slim. So that narrowed it down to all the tall, slim supernaturals in town. So helpful. And frankly, I wasn't even sure I trusted my judgment on that assessment considering how shaky I was from the under-the-door trick.

A sigh of frustration slipped out as I slumped against the door in disappointment. I stayed there for a moment, my head not quite done spinning.

Whoever it had been, they'd moved quickly and kept their head down. As my vision came back to normal, the thought made me look up. Were there security cameras? I glanced around the street. Nothing that looked like a camera.

Maybe they just wanted to get home and into bed. The idea sounded like perfection. I had a full dayshift ahead of me and then another non-date with Cooper. I'd be running on fumes if I didn't crash soon.

Toly's office was a battle for another day. Or

night. Like tomorrow night. I slogged back into the warehouse and pushed the button for the elevator. While I stood there, I stared at the dark office window. Breaking in had gotten me nowhere. The name of the cleaning service was something my father could have figured out by contacting the Financial Department to sniff through Toly's check register. I felt like a failure. I was no closer to figuring this thing out than I had been two days ago.

Cranky and frustrated, I rode up to my apartment and let myself in. I shucked my clothes, threw on my PJ's then did a quick search for Spider. I found him sleeping on one of the kitchen chairs.

"That's not comfortable, you silly thing." I scooped him up, getting a stinky cat-breath yawn in return, and brought him to bed, settling him on the pillow next to mine. He stretched, then curled even tighter.

Being tired apparently wasn't enough to equal sleep. For me. Spider was comatose. I stared into the dark, watching the shadows and trying to make sense of what I knew. I got nowhere, but I kept at it until my head ached with questions.

I thought about calling Greyson and making another attempt at finding out more about that elevator. Despite what my father had told me, I couldn't believe all that lay under the town's streets was electrical conduits and sewer mains.

If that was true, why so much cloak and dagger?

I opened my eyes to the persistent clanging of one of the worst sounds in the world: my phone alarm. I guess I'd slept after all. I fumbled for the phone, hating the noise but thankful I'd set the alarm, because over-sleeping definitely could have happened.

I kicked it into gear, getting Spider fed, his box cleaned (wow, that cat could poop), then grabbed a Dr Pepper for myself and took it in the shower with me. What? Don't judge.

Clean, dressed and hungry, I ate a couple of donuts with another Dr Pepper while I checked my phone. Two messages from last night that I'd missed.

Cooper had texted the fire station address along with *see you soon* and a winky face.

Greyson had texted a selfie from Insomnia, judging by the background. He was holding a drink and making a very come hither look. On second glance, that was just his normal face. The only note attached to that was *Tomorrow*.

My dating life had never been better. I should have lied about who I was ages ago.

I finished the donut in my hand, dried my hair, did my makeup and locked up behind me.

Juniper was already in the hall. "Morning!"

"Morning." I screwed the top onto my Dr

Pepper and stuck it in my purse. "You're awfully chipper." I smiled. It wasn't her fault I'd had a lousy night.

"Well…" She drew the word out as she made a coy expression. "I might have called this guy I've sort of had a thing for, Pete Cathaway, to see if he wanted to join us at the fund-raiser tonight." She squealed softly. "I hope that's okay. I figured since you'd be hanging out with Cooper, I might as well have a guy there too."

How could I say I'd been hoping Juniper being there meant I wouldn't have to be alone with Cooper? Especially when she'd squealed? Clearly she was excited about seeing Pete. "Yeah, sure." Now it was going to seem like a double date. But I kept my smile in place. I didn't want to dampen her good mood. "So this guy, Pete, you dig him, huh?"

"Dang skippy, I do."

"What's he like?"

We walked to the elevator while she talked.

"He's a pharmacist at the drugstore in town. I know, not the most exciting job, but he's really sweet. He came in to buy Christmas gifts for his nieces and nephews, and we sort of hit it off. Then I pretended to have a cold as an excuse to go see him."

I laughed as the doors opened and we got on. "Nicely played. But if you hit it off, why do you need the excuse?"

She shrugged. "He's a little on the shy side. He's half-fae and while he's got pointed ears and the most beautiful blue-green eyes you've ever seen, that's about all being half-fae has done for him. I think I intimidate him."

"Did he say he'd come tonight?"

She nodded and her smile brightened. "Yep."

"Well, maybe he'll see there's nothing to be intimated by. That you're just an awesome person he should get to know better before someone else snatches your hotness up."

All smiles, she poked a finger into my arm. "Thanks."

"I mean it. Any guy would be lucky to have you."

"You too." She assessed me, her gaze going head to toe. "You're tall, beautiful, smart and funny. If I was a guy, I'd be all over you. Heck, if Pete doesn't work out, I may still ask you out."

I put my hand to my chest and fluttered my eyes as I answered her in my best *Steel Magnolias* Southern accent. "Why, Juniper Trembley, you do know how to flatter a girl."

Laughing like fools, we stumbled off the elevator and straight into Toly's path. That snapped us out of it.

I hoisted my purse strap a little higher on my shoulder. "Morning, Toly."

"Morning, Toly," Juniper parroted.

"Morning, morning, work to do," he muttered as he side-stepped us and kept going into the shop. He had a piece of paper in his hands, and his attention seemed to be focused on it.

Juniper and I looked at each other and shrugged.

We got set up for the day. A very distracted Toly gave us a couple of jobs to do and then disappeared back into his office.

As the first customers drifted in, I nudged Juniper. "What do you think that was all about with Toly?"

"Nothing. He gets preoccupied with stuff all the time. Probably some new toy idea he's working on or a notice about the next delivery coming from corporate. Who knows?"

I glanced back at the warehouse. So long as he hadn't figured out someone had been in his office. Which reminded me that I hadn't relocked the filing cabinet. Hopefully, he'd think he'd just forgotten.

But we only saw him two more times the rest of the day, both times when he came in to assign us more tasks. Mostly me. Lots of stocking and inventory and straightening.

Owen and Buttercup showed up a few minutes before five to spell us. She leaned around to grab her apron. "You missed it, Lilibeth. The werewolves were out in force last night. Howler's was happening." She fanned herself. "Ooo, those wolfy boys are smoking."

"Next time, I swear."

Owen stood a few paces behind, waiting until she moved to reach for his apron.

"How was your dinner, Owen?"

He looked up and blinked a few times, all movement frozen in place like every bit of energy he had was going into answering that question. He must have gone to bed even later than I had, judging by the circles under his eyes. "What was that?"

"Your dinner last night. How was it?"

He blinked some more, put his apron on and straightened. After a long pause, he said, "Good."

Then he shuffled off into the back of the store.

"Don't mind him," Buttercup said. "He's half asleep most of the time because he spends all night online with his hordes running missions or whatever they call it. He's a total gamer. That's all he does outside of working here."

"Well, it's not all he does. He was going out to dinner last night. I saw him leave."

She shook her head. "I don't think Owen's left the building since he got here. If it wasn't for delivery, I'm not sure he'd eat."

"Based on the way he was dressed last night, he looked like he was going to meet someone. Like a date. He had a tie on."

She screwed up her face and looked back at the way he'd gone, jerking her thumb in his direction. "That guy? I would have bet a paycheck he didn't own a tie, forget him knowing how to tie one."

"He probably Googled it," Juniper said.

I glanced over my shoulder. Owen was nowhere to be seen. "He also told me Toly had called him in to make sure he could handle the Snowy Saturday shimmer, in case Toly wasn't there. I got the sense he had to give Toly a demonstration of his magic."

"Amateur." Buttercup crossed her arms over her apron. "Juniper and I know better, don't we?"

I peered at her. "You mean Toly's asked you guys that already?"

Juniper nodded. "He usually gets around to it within the first couple months after an employee arrives."

"But those kinds of skills are detailed in our files. Why would he need to ask again?"

Buttercup shrugged. "Because he's forgetful? Because he doesn't trust corporate? Because he checks everything twice? Pick one. Either way, Juni and I both faked it when he called us in."

Juniper gave a little half-grin. "I didn't really fake that much. I told him the best I could do was icicles that had no guarantee of being around longer than five minutes." She snorted. "He scratched me off his shimmer list pretty fast."

"But with hair that color, he had to know you were lying."

She tipped her head forward. "Take a closer look at my roots."

I did. They were dishwater brown. "You color your hair?"

She lifted her head. "Yep. In this day and age, and especially in this town, why not?" She must have read the expression on my face. "It wasn't my magic that got me here. It was my people skills."

So much for my theory that you had to have a certain level of magical skill to work here. "You are better with customers than anyone else I've seen." I glanced at Buttercup. "Don't tell me that yours isn't real either."

"Nope, this is all mine."

I narrowed my eyes at her. "Then you must have skills."

Her lids went droopy with how much she cared. "I do, but I don't want to get stuck handling the shimmer by myself. I told him my gifts are unpredictable. And to prove it, I accidentally" — she made finger quotes around the word — "filled his office with snow in about five seconds."

I would have paid money to see that. "I guess if I get called in I should do the same thing."

Buttercup nodded. "Unless you want to be the Big Elf in Charge on Snowy Saturday, I'd say hells yeah."

Juniper let out a little gasp, then grabbed my arm. "Look at the time. We need to bounce. We have to get ready for the spaghetti dinner."

Ah yes, the non-date and the maybe date. "Yep, let me grab my purse. See you later, Buttercup."

She waved us off. "Later. Have fun with the fire hoes." Then she snorted. "See what I did there? Fire hoes? *Hose*?"

"Yeah, yeah," we said, but we were laughing as we left.

Twenty minutes later we were on the street, headed to the fire station, looking as chillacious as possible with twenty minutes of prep time. Which, if I do say so myself, was pretty freaking chillacious.

I glanced over at Juniper, who was wearing a cute purple dress and boots. "We clean up good."

She nodded. "Yeah, we do."

I'd stuck with skinny jeans, boots and a flannel shirt over a lace-trimmed tank top. My version of country chic. And once again, trying for cute but not too cute. "Pete's meeting you there?"

"That's what he said. I hope he doesn't back out. Hang on, I better check that there weren't any pharmacy emergencies."

"Is that a thing?"

"It can be." She pulled her phone from her purse. We both stared at it. "Nope," she said. "No text from him so I guess we're still on."

"Isn't this an unexpected pleasure?"

The warm honey-over-gravel voice brought my head up in time to stop myself from running smack into Greyson. Whoa. Talk about unexpected. "Oh, hi. Hey." I shuffled nervously, feeling a little like a kid caught lying. Not that I'd lied about anything this time. Or had any reason to feel guilty.

"Lilibeth. How are you?"

"Good, thanks." His gaze shifted to Juniper as his brows rose. Oh, right. "This is my friend Juniper. We work together. We're going to the spaghetti dinner fund-raiser at the fire station."

He nodded. "Sounds...filling." Then he smiled that bone-melting grin of his at Juniper. "A pleasure to meet you, lovely Juniper. Any friend of Lilibeth's is a friend of mine."

But no kiss to the hand. Maybe he was afraid of scaring her. She was looking at him with a slightly bug-eyed expression. Or maybe I was special. I know, long shot, but everyone liked a little ego stroke now and then.

"You, too," Juniper managed.

"You're working?" I asked as I remembered he'd already told me he was on the schedule Friday night. He was dressed pretty much the same as he'd been the night I'd met him. Although he seemed to be wearing a touch of black eyeliner this evening. Very Depp.

He nodded. "VOD until midnight." Then his sly

smile was all for me. "But don't worry, not tomorrow night."

I swallowed. "Okay, well, we should get going."

His gaze lingered on my mouth for a long moment, sending hot little sparks of anticipation through me. "Have fun."

"Thanks. See you...later." I grabbed Juniper's arm and got us moving. It was that or conjure up my own personal snowstorm to put out the fire in my pants.

Five steps in and she found her voice again. "You know Greyson Garrett?"

"Sort of. I mean, I know him well enough that we've shopped for cat litter together." Maybe not one of the finer points in my history of male-female relations, but there it was.

"Then you know he's a" — she lowered her voice — "vampire."

"Yep. I know." Boy, did I. You didn't forget jumping two stories with someone. "Is that not cool for some reason? Aren't we equal opportunity daters?"

"You're dating him?" Her eyes widened again, and her voice went a little screechy. "What about Cooper?"

"Cooper doesn't want a relationship." And neither did I. Not with him, of all people. "And who says I can't keep my options open? Guys date around all the time."

That seemed to calm her down. She nodded. "That is true. But *Greyson*."

"What's so wrong with Greyson?"

She got a curious look on her face. Sort of like someone had just handed her a sex toy and asked her to explain how it was used. "He's…so…*sexy*. And he's a vampire. They're like wild things. Feral."

"Have you had this talk with Buttercup about the werewolves? Because she seems to be a pretty big fan of men with lycan tendencies. And I don't think you get much wilder than a guy who can turn into a wolf whenever he wants. Just saying."

Juniper let out a huge sigh and rolled her eyes. "Yes, I've talked to her about that. You two are so alike."

I took that as a compliment. Buttercup was pretty rockin'.

Juniper shook her head. "Doesn't he scare you?"

I lifted one shoulder in a non-committal shrug. "A little. I think that's part of the appeal."

"Huh, yeah, bad boys." She crossed her hands through the air like she was cutting that thought off at the root. "Not me. I like nice guys with good jobs who aren't ever going to accidentally bite me."

"Like Cooper."

She frowned. "Like Pete."

"Right. Like Pete." Because Cooper *might* bite me when he found out who I really was.

We managed to get to the firehouse about ten minutes early, but it was still pretty busy. Juniper decided to stand outside and wait for Pete, which left me on my own to venture in and look for Cooper.

Volunteers from the school were in last-minute mode, rushing around the rows of tables that had been set up in the big space. I found Cooper hauling in a rolling cart of chairs.

He greeted me with a smile. "You made it."

"No way I was going to miss a chance to slide down your pole." Wait. What had I just said? Heat flared through my cheeks. I looked around to see if there was a sudden sinkhole I could jump into. "I, uh, I mean, the firehouse's pole."

Cooper laughed. "I knew what you meant." But he was still smiling more than necessary. He parked the cart and gestured toward the back of the station. "This way."

"I'll follow you." That way I wouldn't have to look at him. Of course, my gaze became oddly fixated on his butt. Fireman uniforms were well cut, that's all I'm saying.

We went up a flight of stairs in the back of the station and came out in a large room set up dormitory-style with three sets of oversized bunk beds. The back wall was a row of tall single lockers, each with names on them. Across from the bunks was a lounge area with a big wraparound sectional couch, a couple of recliners and a massive flat-screen TV. Man cave central.

And there in the corner, with a semi-circle of railing around it, was a bright, shiny brass pole.

He spread his arms out. "Welcome to our home away from home. This is where we live when we're on shift. The kitchen and dining hall are downstairs, but trust me, you don't want a tour of them right now. Not with the PTA volunteers in there about to serve spaghetti to three hundred people."

"I don't want to be in the way. Or get covered with sauce." I lifted my brows and tipped my chin toward the pole. "Where does that end up?"

"Other side of the dining hall in the ready room. That way, if there's a call, we slide down and are instantly at our gear, ready to suit up and head out."

"Cool."

"So…" He grinned. "Ready to do it?"

I wasn't so sure now. "Is there any trick to it?"

"Sure, watch. I'll show you." He went over and grabbed the pole with both hands, then wrapped his legs around it. He clung there. "See what I'm doing with my legs? How they're bent around the pole? That's how you control your descent."

I nodded. "I can do that."

"Good. Then put the pole in the crook of your dominant arm and keep it close to your body. Use your non-dominant hand higher up to steady yourself. Release your feet a little and down you go."

"Okay." But I didn't get any nearer.

He squinted at me. "You're sure you can do this?"

I made my feet take me close enough to lean over and look down past him. The next floor seemed about a hundred feet away. Why had I thought this was a good idea? "Yeah. I think so."

"Don't chicken out on me."

I just stared at him. I could do this. Couldn't I? What were the chances of dying? Or breaking something?

"You're chickening out on me."

I straightened, trying to find my inner warrior or whatever. "No, I'm not." I was not going to look like a scaredy cat in front of Cooper Sullivan. "You're just clogging up the pole."

"See you at the bottom." He took his hand

off the pole, gave me a little salute and slid down.

Fast.

The knot in my throat was competing with the ice in my stomach to see which one could make me pass out first. No, no, no. I could do this. It was just like jumping off the fire escape with Greyson, except a little less scary because I knew what was coming next.

Frankly, I'd preferred the not knowing with Greyson.

I reached out and grabbed the pole. Wow, that was a long way away.

"Don't worry, I'll catch you," Cooper shouted up from below.

He stood right next to the pole. That was kind of reassuring. If I fell, I'd land on his dumb head. That would serve him right for ditching me all those years ago.

Anger was a good motivator.

I jumped onto the pole, instantly regretting it. I couldn't even suck in a breath to scream. Then Cooper's arms were around me and I was on the ground. I thought about kissing the floor, but that might cost me some cool points.

"You actually did it!"

"Of course I did. What did you think? I was going to back out?" I feigned as much nonchalance as I could muster. Which was way more than I was feeling.

"A lot of people can't do it. Fear of heights and all that."

"Yeah, well, not me." Granted, I was shaking, but let's call that adrenaline. He was still holding on to me. Normally, I'd be unhappy about that, but I'd let it go another couple of seconds, considering the circumstances.

"Well, I'm impressed."

"Thanks." We were all alone in the ready room. Just us and rows and rows of firefighting gear.

He leaned in like he was going to kiss me.

I pulled out of his arms. "I should go find Juniper. I'm sure she's looking for me."

His eyes still held intent. "She's a grown woman. She'll manage."

I put my hand on his chest. "Cooper, you told me you weren't interested in a relationship."

He looped a strand of my hair around one finger and gave it a tug. "Maybe I changed my mind. Maybe *you* changed my mind."

Yeah, and his mind would change again when he found out who I was.

A couple of firefighters walked through, giving him the eye like they knew what he was up to. That was the break I needed. "I'm going out to find Juniper and get a seat. Are you coming or not?"

He nodded, looking less than happy. But that couldn't be helped. I really didn't want to lead him on and make things worse in the end.

He sighed. "I'm coming. I already have seats reserved for us."

"That was nice of you." It really was. But then Cooper had always been that way. Up until he decided we couldn't be a couple anymore.

"We'll have to add one for Juni's date. Who is he?" Cooper held the door back into the main hall. The noise level had kicked up a notch since I'd first gotten there.

"Pete Cathaway. He's a pharmacist. You know him?"

"No, but I've heard her mention him." He scanned the crowd. "I see her. She's in front of the second table of raffle baskets. You want to get her and I'll see about adding a place for Pete? We're at the back table, right hand corner."

"Got it. See you in a minute."

We parted, and I made my way through the crowd, waving at Juniper to get her attention. She waved back and subtly pointed at the guy beside her. He was very handsome in a sort of academic way, something that was only reinforced by the tan chinos, plaid shirt and suit vest he wore. If he and Juniper ever really became a thing, he'd probably write sonnets about her. I liked him already.

She grabbed my hand as I reached them. "There you are."

"I went down the fire pole."

"You did not."

"I did. Scared the pants off me."

She laughed. "I bet Cooper liked that."

"Yeah." I laughed too. "So this is Pete?"

She nodded a little nervously. "Pete, this is my friend Lilibeth I was telling you about."

He nodded in greeting and shook my hand. "Nice to meet you."

"You too." He really did have gorgeous eyes. "Cooper's got seats for us. Follow me." By the time we made it there, dinner was being served.

We sat down and ate. Between the spaghetti and the noise, there wasn't a lot of chit-chat going on, and when there was, most of it was between Pete and Cooper, who'd discovered they both liked trout fishing.

Good for them.

Juniper and I finished eating, then left the boys at the table to get some raffle tickets. I was happy to see they took credit cards so I made a significant purchase. I'd have to remember to tell my dad it was a tax deduction.

Juniper and I stood in front of the table trying to decide which baskets we wanted the most.

I pointed my tickets at the enormous ivory and gold wrapped one. "I think the spa package."

"Hmm. That would be fun. And it's for two." She glanced it me. "We could put the same number of tickets in and if one of us wins it, we promise to take the other person."

"I'm game. How many tickets?"

"Ten." She'd bought twenty.

"I'm in." I'd bought—or rather, my father had bought a hundred. I stuck more than half of mine in and didn't say anything. A day at the spa with Juniper would be the most fun ever. I really hoped we won.

We stuck the rest of our tickets here and there, including in baskets giving away four weeks of ballroom dancing lessons, a collection of twenty signed romance novels (reading is huge in the NP) and a custom cake from Delaney's Delectables. I figured if I won that, I'd bring it into work and get my fellow employees sugared up for a day.

Juniper nudged me. "What do you think of Pete?"

"He's handsome and smart and I think you guys are perfect together."

She beamed. "Thanks. I really like him."

We went back to the baskets for a minute until she grabbed my arm. "I think Cooper's looking for you. I better get back to Pete."

"Okay." Cooper was headed in my direction. Maybe now was a good time to see if he could introduce me to the sheriff. If the sheriff was here. I put on a bright smile.

"Having fun?" he asked.

"You know what? I am. A lot of fun. Juniper and I are winning all of this stuff, by the way."

"You are, huh? Even that evil-eye quilt?"

"Um, no. I didn't spend any tickets on that." I grimaced at the quilt hanging from the firehouse wall. It was literally a giant blue eyeball on a field of rainbow squares. "I couldn't sleep with that thing in my house."

He laughed. "It's supposed to ward off evil."

I took the opening. "I'll let the sheriff do that. Speaking of, did you ask him about the missing employees?"

"No, I haven't had the chance. Haven't seen him."

"Did he come tonight? You said he and your chief are related, right?"

"Yep. Brothers."

"Protecting the town is the family business, huh? Are they vampires too?"

"Nope." He leaned in. "Werewolves. Their sister, Bridget, owns Howler's."

"Get out. Really? I guess that makes sense since you said Ivy was a werewolf too." I looked around for guys who resembled the pretty bartender. "Are they here?"

Cooper nodded. "You want to meet them?"

Did reindeer love carrots? Um, *yes*. But I played it cool. Not at all like I was going to ply them for information as soon as possible. "Sure."

As dessert was being served (standard-issue vanilla sheet cake with chocolate frosting), Cooper led me to a pair of tall, rugged, uniformed men who looked like they'd be very at home in the woods. Outdoorsy types. Which made sense, seeing as how they were werewolves and whatnot.

"Sheriff Merrow, Chief, this is my friend Lilibeth. She's new in town and wanted to make sure it was safe here."

The pair grunted in unison. I took that to be a yes. Or a hello. Hard to tell, as I didn't speak werewolf. "I'm the newest employee at the toy store. Santa's Workshop. You know it?"

The sheriff nodded. "Got my son, Charlie, a remote-control helicopter in there for Christmas. Good stuff. Nice to meet you."

"And welcome to town," the fire chief added.

"Thanks." I shifted my gaze back to the sheriff. "Apparently, there's been a rash of employees quitting at the shop. Just sort of disappearing. You haven't heard anything about that, have you? No unclaimed John Does turning up or a sudden rash of missing-persons reports?"

The sheriff frowned. Then barked out a laugh. "No, ma'am, nothing like that, I promise. But if anything untoward happens over there at the toy shop, you let me know."

He handed me his card.

I took it. "I will, thank you." So much for that.

Cooper shook their hands, then ushered me back to our seats for dessert. "You really think there's something that bad going on at the shop?"

"I don't know. But I can't help but be concerned." We sat. I turned to face him. "What I told you over lunch is true. In nearly three years, six employees have left. Not quit and returned home to the North Pole. They each wrote a note and disappeared. You don't think that's strange?"

He thought for a moment. "That's definitely weird." His eyes narrowed. "Do you think you could be in some kind of danger? Because I'll go back and get the sheriff right now, and we'll —"

Touched by his concern, I put my hand on his arm. "No. I don't think I'm in any danger. But I can't help but wonder what's going on."

He nodded. "I'd hate for something to happen to you."

I smiled. He was sweet. And gorgeous. And built. I took a long drink of my water, which was already iced saving me the trouble of working my magic. "Thank you." Maybe his concern was my chance. "You're a town employee, right?"

"Right."

"Have you ever used that special elevator in the vestibule?"

"Sure."

I almost fell off my seat. "You have? To do what?"

His mouth curved in a reluctant smile. "I can't talk about it. That's a restricted area."

Hello, brick wall, we meet again.

I sighed and stuffed a forkful of cake into my mouth in an attempt to make myself feel better. It worked a little.

He laughed. "Lilibeth, I really can't talk about it. I signed a confidentiality agreement."

I'd heard that before. I smiled weakly. "Don't give it another thought."

His expression turned serious. "You think whatever's going on with the employees has something to do with that elevator? Because I'd doubt that very much."

"No. I don't know. I just think anything's a possibility." I didn't really think the elevator was tied in. How could it be?

"You know only town employees can access it."

"I've heard."

He leaned back and tapped the badge hanging off his utility belt. "You can't even call the thing without swiping an official town keycard programed with the right permissions. No one at the shop would have one unless they also worked for the town. Did any of the employees that quit work more than one job?"

I gave the card a quick glance. It displayed his picture, his name, a town seal and a wide black stripe like a credit card. "Not that I'm aware of." But I'd be checking the files again when I got home tonight, that was for sure.

The overwhelming sense of disappointment I'd had last night returned. I stuck my fork into my cake and stared blindly into the crowd. I needed to talk to my dad, maybe see if just going over everything we knew would help me make sense of something.

My eyes focused on someone in the crowd. I nudged Cooper and pointed with my cake-encrusted fork. "There's that woman from the park."

"Who?"

I got Juniper's attention. I still hadn't figured out where I knew the woman from, but it was bugging me like a loose tooth I couldn't keep my tongue off of. "Hey, see that woman in the jeans and the pink sweater? Short blond hair? Is she a regular customer?"

Juniper swiveled in her seat. She shook her head. "Not that I recall."

I started to get up and go after the woman, but she disappeared in the crowd that was headed out. I exhaled a frustrated breath as I sat down. I didn't even feel like finishing my cake. I was ready to go home. But for Juniper's sake, I put on a happy face.

A man in a sport coat got up and tapped a microphone, causing a squeal of feedback that made everyone cringe and laugh. "Now that I have your attention..." He chuckled nervously. "Sorry about that. Thank you to everyone who came out to support the school. We really appreciate it. And now, we're going to do the basket drawings."

Everyone cheered, and Juniper smiled at me and crossed her fingers. It wasn't that big of a surprise when they read off the number of one of my tickets as the winner of the spa package.

Juniper let out a happy yelp. "You won!"

"*We* won," I corrected her. "Next day off, we're there."

One of the volunteers brought the basket to me and checked my ticket number. The thing was half the size of Juniper and filled with about fifty pounds of lotions and balms and body butter and toner and cleanser and a ton of other stuff I couldn't use up in a year if I showered every day.

Cooper's eyes widened. "That is some basket."

"Worth every penny." I'd be sure to let my dad know his money had been well spent. "I might have to take a cab to get it home, though."

I could lift the thing, I just wasn't sure I could see over it.

"I'll carry it home for you," he said.

"Thanks." That might give me another shot at quizzing him about the elevator, but at this point, I wasn't sure I cared about that stupid thing anymore.

Juniper peeked around the side of the basket. "Since Cooper's going to help you with the basket,

Pete and I are going for a walk. I'll see you at work tomorrow. Cool?"

"Cool." I was happy for her. She deserved a nice guy. And Pete was about as far into the nice guy category as you could get.

As they left, Cooper and I headed out too. The air probably felt chilly to him, but it felt like summer to me.

"Which way?" I asked.

He tipped his head around the swathe of ribbons tying off the top of the basket and nodded to the left. "Main Street is that way."

So was Greyson. I decided to head us in a different direction to avoid a possible testosterone show down. Which might be kind of hot, but I wasn't interested in pitting these two guys against each other. "Can we go a different way? You know, so I can learn more of the town."

"Sure." He went right, and I followed at his side.

We walked without talking for a block, and I was happy to continue like that, but he cleared his throat and broke the silence.

"You think something bad is going on at the toy store. How bad?"

"Bad enough that employees are leaving."

"Could be that manager. I've heard Juniper and Buttercup talk about him. He seems like he might be tough to work for."

I nodded. "Yep. Could be."

"But you don't think so."

"I don't know what to think."

He went quiet for a long time before speaking again. "If you haven't figured anything out by the start of next week, I'll see what I can do about telling you more about the elevator."

A chance at the elevator was the only reason I agreed to let Cooper carry the basket all the way up to my apartment. Plus, he was already on the approved list, so there was that. But seriously, his potentially helping me with the elevator was the biggest break I'd had since I'd arrived.

Which was sad, because it was still just a possibility, not a definite.

He put the spa basket on my kitchen counter and looked around. "Nice place. It's just like Juniper's and Buttercup's."

"I suppose they all look the same except for the bigger apartments on the third floor."

Spider came running out from the bedroom, meowing for food.

Cooper squatted down to greet him. "Hey, buddy, what's your name?"

I leaned on the counter, watching. "I haven't

gotten around to teaching him to speak yet. His name is Spider."

"Aren't you a handsome fellow?" Cooper scratched Spider's head and squinted at me. "You named your cat Spider?"

"I inherited him with that name." I shrugged. "He seems to like it all right. I'd hate to change it and give him some kind of identity crisis."

Cooper scratched him some more. Spider's eyes were closed, his purring cranked up to eleven like Cooper's affections were the best thing he'd ever experienced. Yeah, okay, they weren't awful, but still. Spider could have liked him a little less. But Cooper had always had a way with animals. It was one of the things that had made me fall for him.

"Hey," I said. "Don't go trying to make my cat like you more than he likes me."

Grinning, Cooper stood. He stared at me for a long moment. It was a little unsettling. "You know, you remind me of someone."

I laughed, trying to cover the sudden onset of nerves. "I get that all the time."

He walked over and planted his hands on the counter, framing me in his arms. That left about three inches between us, chest to chest. Not nearly enough for proper airflow. Then he leaned in closer. "I know it's just my mind playing tricks on me, but I feel like I know you better than I really do."

"Is that why you agreed to tell me about the elevator?"

The right corner of his mouth quirked up. "I said I might."

I shrugged like it didn't matter. "I don't know what the big deal is about that thing. It's just an elevator."

"I could say the same thing to you. What's it matter? That elevator doesn't have anything to do with toy store employees leaving. How could it?" He laughed, a deep throaty sound that sent a shiver through me. "You winter elves are so nosy."

"Why? Did Buttercup and Juniper try to get you to tell them about it too?"

He shook his head, his eyes lit with a dark, wicked gleam I remembered very well. He was going to kiss me.

I did *not* want that. Except I sort of did. I closed my eyes and groaned at the battle going on in my head.

Cooper must have read that as me being all swoony with need, because a second later his hot mouth was on mine.

Warmth seeped through me from that single point of contact as though I'd drifted into a sunbeam. It spiraled into me, slow and lazy, turning my bones soft with the kind of languid heat normally brought on by an August afternoon.

Damn summer elves.

My hands went to his chest and I was about to push him off when I realized doing that might ruin my chances at finding out about the elevator.

Also, he was an amazing kisser. I let the kiss go on a little longer, because I'd kind of missed them. Even if the jerk had dumped me. Good kissing was good kissing. But letting this happen was only making things worse, and no matter how we'd ended in college, using him now wasn't right. Even if my end game was solid.

Snowballs.

With a soft sigh, I broke the kiss and pushed him away. "I can't do this, Cooper. I like you." Sort of. "But I can't be more than friends with you." And even that would take some doing once he knew who I really was.

He took a step back and bent his head, whether in disappointment, anger or regret, I couldn't tell. Knowing him, though, anger wasn't likely, but without being able to see his eyes, I wasn't sure.

I was about to say something placating, when over his shoulder, I caught a glimpse of the snow globe on the side table. A blizzard stormed inside the glass bowl. Nice timing, Dad.

"Look, Cooper, thanks for everything, but I should really get to bed. It's been a long day, and I have work in the morning."

His head came up, and he finally looked at me. "I know you."

I froze, stuck between panicking and deciding if I should tell him the whole truth before this got really ugly. "What—"

"I mean, I know your type. You've been hurt before. I get it. I've been hurt too."

I exhaled and nodded quickly. Good enough for me. "That's right. That's why I just want to be friends."

He stuffed his hands in his pockets. "Exactly. We need to get to know each other. Take things slow. I shouldn't have kissed you. It wasn't the right time. I'm sorry."

Now I felt like a heel. "No, it was fine. But yes, too soon. Don't feel sorry about it, okay? It was a good kiss." Too good. I hadn't really wanted to stop. On the side table, snowmageddon raged on. "Thanks for tonight. I had a great time."

He smiled. Crisis averted. "Me too. See you soon?"

I nodded. "Definitely."

His smile stayed in place as he let himself out.

The door closed and I bolted the lock, then ran for the snow globe and pressed the button. "Hey, I'm here."

My dad's face appeared. Looked like he was in his office at the house. "Hi, honey. Did I catch you at a bad time? You look flushed."

"Must be the lighting." Not the kissing. "I was just getting in from a dinner at the fire hall. I met the sheriff and asked him about John Does, that sort of thing. He said there's been nothing, but I also got the sense he thought there wasn't really anything for me to worry about concerning the missing employees."

"That's because he probably doesn't know what we know." My dad's eyes narrowed. "Maybe you should pay him a visit, tell him who you really are and see if that changes his reaction."

"Shouldn't you be the one to do that? You are the Winter King."

"No. That would make this an official inquiry, and I don't want to tip off anyone just yet."

"Okay. I can't go see him tomorrow, and the day after is Sunday, and I don't have any idea if the sheriff works Sunday, but Monday definitely."

"Good." He shuffled some papers. "So I called because I had the Financial Department send me a complete reporting of the Nocturne Falls store. Expenses, overages, the whole lot. I figured that would make it look more like a general inquiry than a targeted search. Anyway, it took some digging, but I found the name of the cleaning service."

I didn't have the heart to tell him I'd already done that after he'd gone to so much trouble. "Great."

He pulled out a sheet of paper. "This is a copy of an invoice. Says Brite Star Cleaners."

I squinted at him. "What's the date on that invoice?"

His gaze shifted. "Last month."

"Okay, something's not right. Is that the only cleaning service he had listed?"

"As far as I know. Why? What's wrong?"

I sighed. "I slipped into Toly's office late last night and did a little investigating on my own."

"Jay, I don't like the sound of that. What if you'd been caught?"

"Then the gig would have been up, I guess. Depends on who caught me. What's the worst Toly could do? Fire me?"

"Let's hope." He shook his head. "What did you find?"

"An invoice for a different cleaning service. Thrifty Maids."

We stared at each other for a second. Then my dad spoke. "He must have fired this one and hired Thrifty Maids."

"Or he's covering something up. I told you, the cleaning service seemed to have completely emptied Bertie's apartment."

"I wish you had some proof."

Spider flopped down on my feet and started rolling around, showing me his tummy. "Maybe I do." I reached down and checked Spider's name tag. Bertie's address and phone number were on the back.

I scooped Spider into my lap so my dad could see him. "Remember how I said I have his cat?"

"Yes."

I held Spider up so his tag was visible. "Bertie's name, address and phone number are on the back of Spider's name tag. So that's proof that his cat was left behind. And the other workers know about Bertie having Spider. At least Buttercup and Juniper do, the two women who also live on this floor."

"But Toly lives upstairs." My dad was catching on.

"Right. If Bertie got Spider after he moved in, maybe Toly didn't know about him." I grimaced. "Or maybe Toly did know about Spider and didn't care. Maybe he was going to pay the cleaning service to get rid of Spider too."

I hugged my little baby closer. I couldn't imagine what might have happened to my boy if I hadn't rescued him. Because make no mistake, he was mine now.

"That makes it seem like Toly's involved in this."

I nodded. "It does."

"Might be time for this to become an official investigation."

"And if Toly finds out and takes off? Or worse? No, Dad, not yet. Let me talk to Juniper tomorrow. See if she knows anything about the cleaning service. There could be a logical explanation. Like you said maybe he recently hired the Thrifty Maids service and fired the other one. Maybe that's why you don't have any invoices from them yet." Except the Thrifty Maids file I'd seen in Toly's office had held more than one invoice. Still, I wasn't ready to jump to conclusions.

"I guess. But that doesn't explain what happened to everything in Bertie's apartment." His gaze shifted to Spider. "I'm willing to give it a few more days, but get that cat a new tag and put the old one in a safe place. We may need it as evidence of just how much Bertie left behind."

"Will do."

"And you be safe too."

I nodded. "I'm not doing anything you wouldn't do."

He snorted out two streams of ice vapor. "That's what I'm worried about. Love you."

"Love you."

My dad's image disappeared and the snow in the globe settled. I gave Spider another hug, then slipped his collar off and pried the tag free before putting his collar back on. "I'm getting you a new tag as soon as I can. This time with my info on it. You cool with that? Being my cat, I mean?"

He rolled over and put his feet on the back couch cushions so he could stare at me upside down.

"I'll take that as a yes. Dinner?"

His ears quivered. Oh, he knew that word.

I got up, tucked his name tag into the zipper pocket of my purse (the only safe place I could think of), then fed him a can of Chunky Chicken Deluxe.

While he snarfed that down, I fixed myself a plate of the last remaining goodies from Delaney's, grabbed a Dr Pepper, and went to the couch to do a little more research. The conversation I'd had with Juniper and Buttercup earlier in the day about magic skills had made me curious, as had the possibility that Cooper had raised about employees having more than one job.

I put my snacks and drink on the coffee table, fired up the TV for company, and retrieved the files I'd brought with me.

Chocolate in one hand, I spread the files out on the coffee table with the other, opening them so I could see each employee's data sheet.

While a rosemary-scented s'more cookie melted over my tongue, I studied the info about the six employees who'd disappeared.

Not a single secondary job that I could see but maybe that wouldn't be listed. I'd have to ask the girls about that.

I read on. The six all had different qualifications. Some had skills in customer service, some had high marks in organization. Bertie had been an exceptional tinker. Not on Toly's level, but very good. Maybe with more time, just as good.

Hmm. Had Toly seen him as competition? If Toly was losing his magic, wouldn't another elf with similar qualifications and strong skills be a threat?

I ran with that idea. But not very far. If my hypothesis was true, and Toly had gotten rid of Bertie, I still had no reason for him to get rid of the other five employees.

Surely they weren't *all* threats.

I popped a coconut bonbon in my mouth, grabbed the first two files and sat back to study them. I reread the employee assessments, finishing up with the magic-skills evaluation. Both were close enough to consider them on the same level.

Repeating the process, I found all six employees to be on par with each other. Which was to say, they were on the higher end of the magic spectrum. And in that respect, on par with the file my father had set up for Lilibeth.

From what I knew about Juniper, having skills that strong wasn't a requirement, but having some magic was. Buttercup was loaded with magic based on her hair color, no matter what she'd told Toly. I had no clue about Owen, but if Toly had talked to him about handling the shimmer, clearly he had strong skills too.

The company definitely preferred a certain skill

level in those it hired for their stores. That explained why the process of getting chosen was so rigorous. Toly had to know that. He had access to these files just like I did. Which meant he had to know Buttercup and Juniper had lied to him about not being able to handle the shimmer.

Unless Juniper really was telling the truth. Her hair color seemed to imply she was, but all elves had *some* magic.

I let out a frustrated sigh. Once again, I was getting nowhere and figuring out nothing. I power walked a couple laps around the living room in an attempt to shed some of the tension building in my muscles.

When I sat down again, I placed the employee assessment sheets next to each other in two rows of three so I could see them all at the same time. I stared at them without really knowing what I was looking for, just letting my mind wander and my eyes glaze over.

Then they focused of their own accord on the picture of the third employee to quit. Franny Isler.

I picked up her sheet and studied it. There was something about her picture. Maybe because her wavy silver locks reminded me of Lark a little bit.

I brought the picture closer. My mouth fell open. Could it be? The realization hit me like a blast of arctic air.

Franny Isler was the woman I'd seen tonight at

the firehouse. The woman I'd seen jogging at the park. Sure, that woman had short blonde hair and her ears weren't pointed, but the face was the same. I'd known that woman seemed familiar but hadn't been able to figure out why.

Until now. I'd been looking at her picture for days in her employee file.

It had to be her. It *was* her. Or a version of her.

But what on earth did that mean?

The only thing that stopped me from getting to work earlier than I did was a round of texting with Greyson to finalize our evening plans. As it was, I beat Juniper to the store by seven minutes and, I think, impressed Toly just a little bit.

Even so, his shaggy white brows pinched together as he stared at me. We were ten minutes from opening, and he was clearly wound up about the day. "You sure you're all ready for Snowy Saturday?" he asked.

Juniper nodded unconvincingly so I chimed in with a loud, "Positive."

Toly studied me. "You really think you're going to be able to handle it? I'd like very much to get these reports done, but if you can't say so now. I can't risk having anything go wrong."

Juniper moved slowly away.

"It's no big deal." I wiggled my fingers. I could

do this in my sleep. "This sort of shimmer is right up my alley. You've got nothing to worry about."

Juniper looked up from straightening a display by the front window to shoot me a look that said she wasn't sure why I was being so up front about my skills.

"I don't usually leave such an important job in the hands of an employee I haven't personally vetted—"

"You've read my file. I can do it."

At last, he smiled. "All right, all right. But you call me if you need help. Owen will take over when he gets in so it's not like you have to run the shimmer all day."

"Got it." The guy was seriously concerned about this.

"I'll be in my office doing paperwork if you need me." He started for the back, then stopped and turned around. "When I say no problems, I mean I expect things to go smoothly. No accumulated snow. No puddles. No damage to the—"

"Toys. I know. It'll be perfect. Promise." I channeled my magic and started the snowfall to show him. Big fat flakes floated down from the ceiling to disappear right before they touched the floor.

He watched for a moment then nodded approvingly and left. That was about the right response. There was nothing negative he could say. Outside of my family, no one could touch the quality of my magic.

Juniper joined me at the register. "You were awfully eager to prove you could handle the shimmer. Mark my words, you're going to be in charge of it every Snowy Saturday now." She shook her head. "Buttercup and I warned you."

"I was trying to get rid of him."

"Well, good job." She reached out and caught a flake. "Nice snow, by the way. These are gorgeous. And fluffy. Oh yeah, he's definitely putting you on the schedule for every Snowy Saturday."

I shrugged. Toly could put me on the schedule for whatever he wanted. I only was here until I figured this thing out. Which reminded me of why I'd been trying to get rid of him in the first place. "Hey, before the madness begins. What do you know about the cleaning service Toly uses?"

She raised her brows. "Um…like what?"

"How long have they been the cleaners here?"

She squinted. "They started not long after I arrived."

So way more than a month. "How do you know?"

She tipped her head like she was thinking. "I'm not sure I would have known except the smell was different. With the first company, my apartment always smelled like lavender on cleaning day. Now it always smells like lemon."

I nodded. I'd noticed the lemon scent. "Does this company clean better than the other one? Could that be why he changed companies?"

"Not sure. They seem the same to me. I'm not really a messy person, though. And no one else has been here long enough to have had the other cleaning service except me. Why the interest?"

I really wanted to confide in Juniper, but I also didn't want to put her in a position that might require her to cover for me should Toly figure anything out. "I just…I can't stop thinking about all the employees that have quit."

Her mouth bent in an incredulous grin. "And you think the cleaning service might have something to do with it? Like they might have accidentally sucked our workers into their industrial vacuums?"

It did sound unlikely when she put it that way. "Not to that extreme, but maybe they're in on it somehow. They did clear out Bertie's apartment."

"Sure, but Toly probably had them do that so the apartment is ready for the next new hire. Bertie's stuff is most likely in storage."

Huh. I hadn't thought of that. Suddenly all my conjecture seemed silly. I was making mountains out of molehills, all in the name of solving this thing.

Didn't explain the change in cleaning services, but it didn't implicate the new service either. Maybe the new cleaning service was cheaper. Maybe Toly was pocketing the difference. I had no idea. My head hurt from how much I didn't know.

Fortunately, we were swamped with customers coming in to gawk at the snow. Very few of them left without buying something, which meant Juniper and I were hopping. When Buttercup came in at noon for the overlap shift, we needed the help. Neither one of us took lunch until after two.

By five, I was wiped out. Handling the shimmer while also taking care of customers and keeping the shop in order was more work than I'd been used to in a long time. Frankly, I could see why Toly needed the break.

Owen took over the shimmer, and Juniper and I clocked out.

In the elevator, I leaned against the wall.

"Tired?" she asked.

I nodded. "And my night's not over yet."

"How come?"

I smiled despite my lethargy. "I have a date with a certain vampire."

"You don't."

"I do. We're going to dinner." And if I was going to get through it, I was in desperate need of a hot shower, a little caffeine and some sugar. Preferably at the same time.

Juniper shook her head. "Well, you have fun. But be careful." Then she grinned. "Pete's coming over with Thai and a movie."

The doors opened and we got out. "That sounds perfect."

We stopped at our respective doors, both digging for our keys. She got hers in the lock then looked at me. "You could always do the same with Greyson. Have him over, I mean."

I pushed my door open. "You think Toly would approve a vampire?"

She laughed. "I have no idea, but I'd like to see his face when you ask."

"Tell me about it. Have fun tonight."

"You too."

About ten minutes after I got into the apartment, I hit the shower, Dr Pepper in hand. The combination did wonders. Thinking about Greyson didn't hurt either. For the half an hour it took me to get ready, I was able to push the problem of the employees to the back burner.

But at some point, the two collided, and I started practicing a speech that would charm Greyson into telling me about the elevator. A speech that involved me promising him *things*.

Of course, then I'd have to deliver if he came through. I liked the guy. A lot. But maybe not so much that I was willing to sleep with him to gain access to secret areas. Not yet anyway.

Or would he rather bite me? There was a thought that hadn't occurred to me earlier, but the man *was* a vampire.

Maybe I could agree to that. One small bite. Body part of my choice. Although maybe I should do some research on vampires before agreeing to anything that involved fangs. You know, just in case one small bite wasn't enough for most vamps.

I ran a slick of raspberry gloss over my lips and stepped back to take in the whole picture. Not bad. He'd said a nice dinner, so I was in a little black dress and heels that would have been sensible if they'd been a half inch shorter. Unlike my evening with Cooper, tonight I was going for sexy.

Irresistible, actually. That way Greyson would be unable to say no to me when I asked him about the elevator again.

I brushed a piece of lint off my dress and went out to stock Spider up on food before I left. I gave him some love as he chowed down, then grabbed my small evening bag and my leather jacket and went to meet Greyson by the warehouse door.

There was no sign of him as I stepped onto the sidewalk.

Then I heard a long, low whistle. I turned toward the sound and saw him walking in my direction.

He wore a dark suit with a crisp white shirt open at the neck. The image of this wild, untamed man in a restrained suit was the most delicious thing I'd seen since the day I'd walked into Delaney's.

The suit fit him perfectly and had no doubt been made for him, but there was something about him in it—maybe the too-long curls or the dark stubble shadowing his face, or the out-of-place excess of silver jewelry—that gave him an air of dangerous, rebellious bad boy.

Or maybe that's just how vampires looked when they dressed up.

He took my hand as soon as he was close enough to reach me, wrapped his strong fingers around mine and lifted them to his mouth for a kiss. His lips lingered there as he spoke. "You look good enough to eat."

A shiver ran through me and I knew he saw it. I tried to play it off. "I bet you say that to all the girls."

"I don't date girls. Just women. And even then, not very often." He held on to my hand as he brought it to his side.

"Are you trying to flatter me?"

"No." His eyes flashed silver. "If I was trying to flatter you, I would tell you that you are the most radiant creature I have ever beheld, and that seeing you looking so beautiful this evening fills me with the desire to spoil you in ways you've not yet imagined." He pulled me closer. "I might even say that while our evening has just begun, I already dream of when I might next have the honor of your company and the pleasure of your hand in mine."

I stared at him, feeling like the elven equivalent of infatuated mush. I was so overcome with feelings I couldn't name that English had become a foreign language. I might have mumbled something. Or maybe I just made a noise.

Either way, he leaned in and brushed a kiss across my mouth. "Good evening, my darling Lilibeth. I trust your day has gone well."

I nodded. Good, I still had movement. I cleared my throat and tried for words. "It was busy."

"Would you rather not go out then?"

"No." I smiled. "I absolutely want to go out." We could stay in another night when we didn't look this hot.

He returned my smile and slipped his arm around my waist. "Then off we go."

We took our time on the walk to the restaurant. Maybe that was Greyson being mindful of my high heels or maybe it was because we were wrapped up in conversation, but either way I was happy for the fresh air.

And the outstanding company.

We even came upon a pet store and got a new tag for Spider. Greyson bought him a little fluffy catnip toy, too, insisting I give it to him when I got home.

If the man was trying to cement a place in my life, he was doing a pretty good job.

I had to admit, Greyson was an experience unlike any I'd had before. As the Winter King's daughter, I'd attended many formal events where I'd been plied with elegant words meant to flatter and turn my head. Most, if not all, of those men had been trying to sway me to buy favor with my father.

But Greyson was just being Greyson. A man who had no reason to be anything other than what he was. It was so refreshing that being with him was like seeing the Northern Lights for the first time.

I was seriously on the verge of falling into deep like with this guy. That worried me a little. Mostly because one of us could end up hurt when I left. And by one of us, I meant me. I hadn't counted on developing feelings for anyone. I hadn't even thought I'd be dating!

But that bridge had been crossed. Now I just had to find an adult way to handle what was happening. I mean, bringing a cat back to the North Pole was one thing. Bringing a vampire home? That might not go over as well.

Of course, I was assuming Greyson would even be interested in visiting. Maybe being with me was just him having fun. Maybe it meant nothing to him.

Maybe that's what I should go with.

Because the last thing I wanted was to get my heart broken again. I'd had enough of that with Cooper.

Dinner was at a little French place called Café Claude. It was dark and intimate and lit primarily by candles and a few dim chandeliers that cast soft prisms of light over everything. Pristine white cloths, gleaming silverware and sparkling crystal adorned the tables. Soft violin music played in the background. If you'd told me we'd suddenly been transported to Paris, I would have believed you.

I couldn't imagine a more perfect spot for dinner with a vampire.

After we were seated and drinks ordered, Greyson took my hand across the table. "Do you like it?"

"It's lovely."

"They just opened a few weeks ago. The owner, Jacque Baptiste, has been a friend of mine for many years."

"Is he a vampire?"

"No. He is a *voyante*."

Greyson's French accent sent a trill down my spine. His normal Irish one was tempting enough, but the French? Dangerous. "I don't speak French, so I don't know what that means." But he could say it again as many times as he liked.

"A *voyante* is a clairvoyant. Jacque gets glimpses of the future. It's not something he can always control, though."

That gave me a moment of pause. "How does that work? Does he have to touch people? Or something they've touched?" Because either way, I might get burned.

"No, they're just visions that come to him. No touching involved. And since he can't control it, the gift does him very little good as far as making money." Greyson smiled. "Fortunately, he's also a very talented chef."

I smiled back in relief. Seemed like I was in the clear. "This town never ceases to amaze me. So who's Claude then?"

Greyson laughed softly. "His little white terrier. The French love their dogs."

Before we got deeper into our conversation, a short wiry man with bright black eyes came to the table. He held out his arms to Greyson and rambled excitedly in French. Jacque, I was guessing.

Greyson answered him in French. I closed my

mouth to keep from drooling. Then he broke into English and introduced me. "My lovely companion, Lilibeth Holiday."

Jacque kissed my hand and smiled brightly. "Lilibeth, it is my pleasure."

"Mine as well."

He released my hand and snapped upright like a soldier awaiting orders. "I will make anything your heart desires."

How sweet. "That is quite the offer. What do you suggest? I'm not picky. In fact, since you're the chef, I leave the decision up to you. I will eat whatever you put in front of me."

He put his hand flat to his chest and sighed. "I am in love." Then he smiled at me. "I will bring you the best dish."

"What about me?" Greyson said.

Jacque fluttered his hand at Greyson. "You will get what you get."

I laughed. "I like this guy."

Jacque took off for the kitchen, and our server showed up behind him with our drinks: wine for Greyson, sparkling water for me. I needed my head clear.

The server left and we were alone again.

Greyson swirled the wine in his glass. "How was your spaghetti dinner last night?"

"Good. Fun. I won one of the raffle baskets. It's a whole spa package." I'd promised to take Juniper, but now I was thinking I might send her with Buttercup in my place. After they found out who I really was, it might help smooth things over.

"Very good. So you're enjoying Nocturne Falls then?"

"I am. This is such a great town."

He swallowed a sip of wine. "It is. There are so few places that people like us can live our lives in the open. This place is a gift."

Too bad I was going to have to return it. "Is that why you work for the town then? Because you want to give back?"

"That, and I want the town to remain successful. Entertaining the tourists does that." He smiled into his wine. "The Ellinghams are also very generous employers."

That perked me up. "What do you mean?"

He shrugged. "They compensate their employees very well. Housing allowances, substantial salaries, discounted store rents, whatever it takes to put the right people in the right positions."

My mind was working faster than I could put into words. "So if they wanted you to work for them, they'd put together a package that would be hard to turn down?"

He nodded. "Absolutely."

Which meant they were very capable of hiring away the store's best employees. But then wouldn't those employees still be traceable? From what my father had said—and the census supported—they had all seemed to disappear. Or was that something the Ellinghams had arranged? A way of protecting the workers they'd poached from being poached back?

But then why would they have said anything to my father about the issue? Unless that was just a way of covering their backsides.

I was so confused. But I also felt like I might be on to something. Something I needed to dig into a little more. "Are they hiring?"

His brows lifted. "Looking to change jobs already?"

"Hey, no reason not to keep my options open, right?"

"Fair enough. You want me to set something up for you?"

"You'd do that?" If I talked to the Ellinghams and showed them what I could really do, like the full extent of my magic, they might make me an offer. I could see for myself if they were behind our missing elves.

"Of course." He smirked. "So long as you're really interested and not just trying to get access to that damned elevator."

"The thought hadn't even occurred to me." It really hadn't. But now that Greyson had mentioned it, this plan had even more merit.

Jacque and the server arrived with our meals. Jacque placed my dish in front of me first. He removed the silver cap with great flourish. "For you, wine-poached salmon with truffles and roasted potatoes."

"Sweet fancy Christmas. It looks and smells amazing." My mouth was watering. I hadn't realized how hungry I was until just now. "I can't wait to taste it."

The server put Greyson's plate before him and backed away. Jacque took the cover off and announced, "For you, steak frites."

Which was basically steak and french fries, but I'm sure there was nothing basic about the way they tasted.

Greyson smiled. "You know me so well, my friend."

Jacque gave us a little bow. "Bon appétit!" And then he left us to it.

The food was amazing, and our conversation became all about just how amazing. We shared bites off our plates, and I was happy my assessment of Greyson's steak and french fries had been right on.

I stole another fry off his plate. "I've never had french fries like this in my life. He must sprinkle them with crack."

Greyson snorted. "Not exactly. But he does fry them in duck fat."

"Seriously?" I reached for another one. "Everything should be fried in duck fat."

"I'm sure that sentiment will make Jacque very happy."

When we'd cleaned our plates and assured Jacque that the meal had been an unparalleled success, we sat for a long time talking. So long, that at least an hour went by before we realized the check had never come.

Grayson asked the server about it, and was told Jacque had taken care of it. When Jacque came out to check on us, Greyson pressed some money into the man's hands. Jacque tried to refuse it, but Greyson was insistent.

"Jacque, take the money. Giving your customers free meals is no way to run a business."

"Ah, but my friend, I already owe you so much."

Greyson's mouth set in a stern line. "Take the money or I will never darken your door again."

I raised my hand. "I will, though. I could eat here every night. Any chance you deliver?"

Jacque beamed. "For you, I could find a way." He clutched the bills but narrowed his gaze at Greyson. "As for you, I will accept the payment. But only because I want to stay on Lilibeth's good side."

I grinned. "All that requires is dessert."

Jacque threw his hands into the air. "Dessert! *Mais bien sûr!* I shall return." He hurried off.

"Now you've done it," Greyson chuckled and tilted his head. "There's no telling what he'll come back with."

"Whatever it is, I'll eat it."

Greyson smiled. "I'm glad we came here. And thank you for your enthusiasm about the food. Jacque needed that."

"I was just telling him the truth. That was easily one of the best meals I've ever had."

His expression softened into something kind and hopeful. "Maybe this should be our Saturday night place."

I didn't know if I'd be here for another Saturday, but how could I say no to that? "I love that idea. But we should take turns paying."

"Good. Then it's done. But we will not take turns paying."

"Why not?"

"Because I am old-fashioned about such matters, and a man should pay when he invites a woman to be his guest."

"What if I was independently wealthy?"

He raised a brow. "I don't see what that has to do with anything. If you were the Queen of England, I would still insist on paying."

I grinned and took his words as a sign. Maybe he'd visit me in the NP after all. "Fine, you've made your point."

Jacque returned with one large plate and two

small ones. The large one held four profiteroles the size of tennis balls. Butter-yellow pastry cream overflowed from their stuffed middles, and a dark chocolate glaze zigzagged over their golden-brown tops.

He put the plate down between us, then gave us each a small one.

"Those look delicious. Too bad you didn't bring Greyson any."

Jacque laughed. "I hope you like them."

"I love profiteroles. They're one of my favorite things." Anything with sugar and chocolate was one of my favorite things, but that was a minor point.

"I am very happy to hear that." He hesitated. "If I may…"

I smiled up at him. "Sure, what is it?"

His expression grew darker. "When I was in the kitchen, I had a vision." He frowned. "I should explain. I see things sometimes. Glimpses of what is to come."

I gulped, hoping hard it wasn't a vision of me as Jayne. "Greyson told me."

"Good," Jacque said. "I have had one about you. I don't know what it means, but I must tell you. It's the only thing that brings me peace."

"What was it?"

"You were in a dark room, and you were in danger. I am sorry to tell you this, but perhaps now you can avoid it. Please, mademoiselle, be careful."

"I will. Thank you." I wasn't sure what to make of that. Toly's office counted as a dark room and I might have been in danger. Maybe his vision had already happened.

He did his little bow again and left us to eat.

Greyson frowned. "I don't like the sound of that at all."

Neither did I, but I couldn't risk making a big deal out of it and tipping Greyson off as to who I really was. I didn't think he'd care that I was the Winter Princess, but the fact that I'd been lying to him? Yeah, that wasn't going to be such an easy sell. "Probably nothing. Maybe he had a vision of me in the middle of the night trying to avoid stepping in one of Spider's hairballs."

Greyson was unamused. "I've never known one of Jacque's visions to be wrong."

I put on my best serious face. "I promise to be careful, whatever I'm doing." I pulled the plate of profiteroles closer.

Seemingly mollified, Greyson cleared his throat and rested his hands on the table. "Will you be sharing those?"

"Maybe." I took one for myself then slid the plate toward him, smiling. "C'mon, join me."

He didn't have to be told twice. Between us we made short work of the cream puffs, and after a long goodbye with Jacque, Greyson and I were back out in the night air.

I looped my arm through his. "That was really nice. Thank you."

"The pleasure was all mine."

"I don't think that's true at all, especially because I had three of the four profiteroles."

He smiled. "You do like your sweets."

"It's a winter elf thing."

His chest puffed out. "I have been told I am *very* sweet."

"Yes, I'm sure all the women tell you that." I squeezed his arm. "You are many things, Greyson. Sweet could be one of them, but it's not the first thing that comes to mind."

His gaze slid sideways. "What is?"

Sexy. But I wasn't sure I wanted to tell him that. "Generous. Kind. Easy to be around."

"Excellent. I sound like someone's grandmother."

I laughed. "How about sexy? I was going to say that first, but I didn't want you to get a big feeling about yourself."

His eyes lit up. "You think I'm sexy?"

"Oh, come on. You know you are." I leaned back to take him all in. "You're like a walking aphrodisiac. You and your manly stubble and piercing eyes. And don't even get me started on the vampire thing."

His lips bent oddly, and I realized he was trying not to laugh. "You are quite the flatterer."

"I learned everything I know from you."

We bantered the whole way home. I couldn't remember when I'd been so at ease with someone, or had time go by so quickly. (Well, maybe in college with Cooper.) I'd checked the time on my watch. It was almost eleven. Hard to believe we'd spent nearly five hours together. It seemed so much less than that.

When we reached the warehouse door, I faced him, and he took both of my hands and stared into my eyes. "My darling elf, when can I see you again? Next Saturday is too far away."

"Toly was working on the schedule today. How about I text you as soon as I know what my next night off is?"

"That will do." He kissed me, softly at first, then with greater insistence.

I leaned into him, kissing him back. The man was as tempting as any dessert I'd ever had, but unlike with most desserts, there was no risk of overindulging. I couldn't get enough of him.

We finally came up for air. His smile was as languid and warm as my insides felt. "I regret that I cannot walk you to your door."

I tipped my head toward the warehouse. "You sort of have."

"Not good enough for me, but what choice do I

have? Unless you'd like me to get you up to the fire escape the same way we came down."

"No, thank you." Not with a full stomach.

He pulled the warehouse door open. "Until the next time."

I kissed him once more on the way in, because I could. "Until then." I made a face at the aftershave aroma that wafted out of the vestibule. "Owen must have just left."

Greyson peered inside. "I don't think so, or I would have smelled that scent out here as we approached." He wrinkled his nose. "And I would not have missed that particular mix of aromas."

"Well, I doubt he was putting aftershave on in the vestibule, so he had to have left this way. Unless…" I stepped inside, put my nose next to the elevator doors and sniffed. "He could have gone down the elevator."

To his credit, Greyson did not roll his eyes as he joined me in the vestibule. He did, however, purse his mouth into a placating expression. "Not without a keycard."

"Maybe he went with somebody who had one."

Greyson shoved his hands into his pants pockets. "I suppose you'd like me to go down and have a look."

"Would you?" Especially if I could tag along.

After a long moment, he sighed. "Yes. But you can't come with me."

Bugger. "I'd be willing to offer you something in return."

His brows shot up. "Something?"

I popped my hip out and put my hand on it in what I hoped was a seductive pose. "I'm sure we could work out a deal."

His eyes glittered. "I don't think you're ready to give me either of the two things I'd like most from you, and when you are ready, I don't want them because of a *deal*."

"Two things? I'm pretty sure I know what one of them is, but the second—"

He bared his fangs at me. "You'll figure it out."

"Oh. You want to bite me."

"That's one." He shook his head in amusement and pulled out his keycard. "You're staying here. I'll only be a few moments."

He slid his card through the reader and called the elevator. Seconds later, the doors opened. He got on and left me standing there, thinking about what it would feel like to have his teeth on me.

In me. Whatever.

I tried to tell myself maybe it wouldn't be so bad, but what did I really know about vampires? Not much. Except this one was smoking hot.

There was no way he could turn me with one bite, was there? I needed to find that out first. I did not want to be a vampire. If that was even possible. And I absolutely got to pick the spot. Hmm. I wondered if that would be enough to entice him into finally showing me where that elevator led.

Maybe I should offer him something else. Something like— Before I could think about it anymore, he was back. He leaned out, holding the doors open. "Get on. You might as well see for yourself."

I jumped onto that elevator with all the speed my little elfy self could muster. I wasn't taking chances in case Greyson changed his mind.

He kept holding the doors open as I joined him, like he might do just that. "You must swear that you will not tell a soul about this."

"I swear. All day long. My lips are sealed."

"Swear on something that holds value to you."

"I swear on my father's crown." *Snowballs.* I should not have said that.

His eyes narrowed. "What does that mean?"

I shrugged and played it off. "It's just an elven expression."

"You understand this could cost me my job." His voice held an edge of seriousness I hadn't heard from him before.

"I do understand. That's the last thing I want. I promise, not a word to anyone."

He pulled his hand back. The doors closed and the car started down.

I had no idea what to expect when the doors opened again, but it certainly wasn't what lay before me.

Greyson held his hand out for me to exit first. "Welcome to the Basement."

"Is that the official name for this place?"

"Yes. But you shouldn't know that."

"Got it." I stepped out into an alcove off of a clean, well-lit hallway that was the breadth of an average street. Small signs on the walls marked directions, and lines on the floor divided the space into two throughways. "Looks like a road."

"It is. Sometimes."

The alcove we were in was darker, but not too much. Two doors flanked either side of the elevator, both with keypads keeping them off-limits. "What's in those rooms?"

He shrugged. "Above both our paygrades, but probably just storage." He lifted his brows. "You smell what I smell?"

I inhaled. There was a faint chlorine smell, but definitely nothing remotely like sewer. And more distinctively, Owen's cologne. "The same aftershave. Owen was down here. But he's not now. Is that why you brought me down here?"

"Essentially. I thought it would put an end to all

the questions if you realized there wasn't anything to see."

I looked around, but there was no way to know where he'd gone or what he was doing down here. "He could have gone down one of the halls."

"He didn't. The scent ends here. I think he came down, looked around and went back up."

"Same as I did."

Greyson nodded. "You elves are a curious lot."

I guess we were. And Owen's curiosity definitely fell in line with my theory about the town making the elves disappear because they'd snooped. Didn't bode well for Owen.

Or me. *Snowballs.* "Are you going to say anything to anyone about him being here?"

"Not about you or him. For all I know, he could have been brought here by one of the Ellinghams. He might even be secretly working for the town. You never know about things like that in Nocturne Falls."

Which brought me back to my father's original theory that someone might be poaching workers. And in this case, that someone had to be the Ellinghams. "Understood. And look, I don't want you getting into any trouble for this. I truly don't. I know it was a risk for you, and I really appreciate you doing that for me."

He gave a little nod. "I trust you, Lilibeth."

Which made me feel lousy for not telling him the truth about who I was, but I couldn't waste too much time on that feeling. Not while I was finally getting somewhere on this case.

My first impression of the Basement was a little anti-climactic, but at least my curiosity had been satisfied. Sewer and electric. Hah. Wait until I told my father about this. Except, technically, I couldn't because I'd promised Greyson I wouldn't say a word to anyone. "Why is it called the Basement? That sounds so official."

"It's just what the place is called."

"But why would town employees need to come down here?"

"I can't answer that."

I sensed I might be wearing out my welcome but I couldn't stop myself. Not yet. "You know, Owen had a date the other night. I wonder if that date was with someone who works for the town. Maybe that's who brought him down here. Is there anywhere in this Basement you'd take a date to impress them?"

Greyson tilted his head as though that question answered itself. "As all town employees sign an NDA, I'd have to say absolutely not. I doubt anyone would risk their job to impress a date."

"Oh right, the non-disclosure agreement. Well, it was worth a shot." I started toward the end of the alcove so I could look down the hall in both directions and get an idea of what else went on down here.

Greyson's hand on my arm stopped me. "This is the end of the tour, sorry, my lovely. I know you'd like to spend the rest of the evening down here snooping around, but—"

"Hey, I don't snoop." Oh, I totally snooped. "I investigate."

"Whatever you call it, it's over." He stepped to the side and gestured back toward the elevator. "Please."

I walked on without another word. He'd been more than generous to bring me down here. I didn't want to give him reason to never do it again. Or to be cross with me.

We rode up and kissed good night one more time in the vestibule, then I went to my apartment.

As I changed into my pajamas, I thought about what to tell my father. If the Ellinghams were behind this, what would that mean for the store? Most likely, the end. My dad and uncle Kris would shut it down.

Or worse, the Ellinghams might retaliate for being called on their poaching and kick the company out of Nocturne Falls. (And if they were in the process of poaching Owen, what on earth did they want him for?) If they could take the building away from the company because someone there messed with the elevator, they would definitely take it away if they found out I'd been down here. And how else would I explain what I'd found out?

Neither outcome was good. And both resulted in no more Santa's Workshop, which meant Juniper and Buttercup would be out of jobs. Sure, Toly and Owen, too, but I'd feel the worst about the women. They were friends. I had so few of those, I wanted to protect them. Even if they decided they were done with me after my true identity came out.

I sat on the bed, trying to sort things. Spider jumped up beside me. I scratched under his chin. I couldn't tell my dad yet. Not until I had proof. Otherwise, I might be starting something that didn't need to be started.

Once again, I had more questions than answers. So I did the only thing I could. I went back to the employee files, searching for something I'd missed.

First, I grabbed a Dr Pepper. Then I fished the fluffy catnip ball out of my evening bag and tossed it to Spider. He leaped on it with great enthusiasm, flinging it into the air and then picking it up and tearing around the house with it. "Your uncle Greyson will be so happy to know you liked his gift."

While Spider got further looped on nip, I spread the files on the coffee table and studied them in the hopes that a missed detail would pop out.

Ten minutes into my fruitless efforts, Spider skittered across the coffee table and sent everything flying in a snowstorm of paperwork.

"Dude!" At least the cap was on my soda. Papers floated down around me as I bent to pick up the mess. "Crazy animal."

Everything was out of order. I scooped the whole lot into a pile and sat on the couch to sort it. The first three sheets were resignation letters from the employees. I started to put them into the files where they belonged, then stopped.

I flipped through them, looking closer. Was this the small detail I'd missed? I found the other three and compared them. These were just copies, and not great ones, but I knew Toly still had all the originals.

Copying the letters had caused a watermark on the paper to show up due to the higher contrast. I hadn't noticed it on the ones I'd seen in Toly's office, but now I could pick out a faint triple A mark on the lower corner.

Of every letter.

How was it possible that they'd all been written on the same brand of paper? Was it company issued? Was it the brand used in the store? That could be. Or was it the brand of paper the Ellinghams used?

I held one of the letters up to the light. Two watermarks became visible. One that had shown up because of being copied and the real one that was in the paper itself. One overlapped the other due to the copied letter being not quite straight when it had been on the machine. In Toly's office. He'd made these copies.

What were the chances that each employee had just happened to write their resignation letter on the same brand of paper Toly used in his copier?

I was guessing pretty slim. Time for more snooping.

I changed out of my pajamas and into my ninja burglar outfit, grabbed my phone, and went back downstairs. There was no hesitation in me as I slipped beneath Toly's office door. I stood, eyes closed for a moment to let the dizziness subside, then I brought my phone to life and navigated to the filing cabinet.

I repeated my ice pick trick and pulled the second drawer open. There, in the back half, were the past employee files. I pulled all six out and studied the letters one by one. The ink colors were different, the handwriting was different, but even by the dim light of my phone, I could tell the paper was the same. Same feel, same watermark, same color.

How had none of us noticed this before? Well, Dad and I had seen only copies, so it wouldn't have raised a red flag that the letters were all on the same paper since they'd all been run through the same copier. And whoever handled the resignation letters after they were found probably wouldn't have noticed because the six letters had been spaced out over the course of two and a half years.

But it would help to have some confirmation. I looked around Toly's office for his copier. Once I found it, I picked my way through the piles of stuff to open the supply tray and take out a sheet of paper.

Yep, same stuff.

So this was company issued. Had to be. Toly was a company man. Seemed logical that he'd use what was sent to him. There was no reason to go out and buy anything else.

But that didn't explain why employees who had just up and decided never to work at the store another day in their lives had used this paper to write their departure letters on.

If I decided to do the same thing, where would I get paper? I'd use what I had, which was that spiral-bound notebook I'd bought at the Shop-n-Save. Had none of the other employees had a notebook or anything?

Let's say that was the case. A huge long shot, but I was going with it. How had they ended up with the same paper? No way would they have broken into Toly's office just to write an I'm-out-of-here note. But we all had keys to the store.

I straightened up in Toly's office, folded the sheet of paper from the copier and stuck it in my hoodie pocket, then slipped back into the warehouse.

Once I was steady on my feet, I let myself into the store with my key. After working here, I pretty much knew where most of the supplies were kept. But I didn't spend a lot of time behind the counter on the register. That had to be where the paper was.

The counter was a maze of cubbies and drawers. Using my phone for light again, I kneeled behind the counter and started searching. Besides the stacks of merchandise bags in three sizes, I found register tape, pricing guns and rolls of stickers, a box of rubber bands, an out-of-date phone book, gift card envelopes, a spiral-bound notebook with most of the pages ripped out, and the secret stash of candy.

There was also a small cardboard box marked Lost and Found. It contained a cell phone, several pairs of sunglasses, three pacifiers (ew), and a set of earbuds.

The drawers held scissors, tape, pens, markers, paperclips, a tin of breath mints, and a bunch of takeout menus. The normal flotsam and jetsam of retail life.

But none of the paper that was in Toly's office.

I sat back on my heels. I hadn't searched every inch of my apartment to see if there was some sort of stationery welcome pack, but I hadn't run across anything in my day-to-day life. And if there had been, wouldn't it be more of a simple notepad like you got in a hotel room? Chances were good I already knew the one and only place to get that paper.

Had the employees come to Toly first? Tried to work things out, maybe? A last-ditch effort to solve whatever was driving them to leave. That could explain how all of their letters were written on that paper. He'd have asked them to put something in writing, something to go in their file.

That was plausible.

But it didn't erase the feeling that Toly was somehow responsible for this. I tipped my head back and sighed. Without proof, what did I have? Guesses and hunches and speculation. None of which got me any closer to my goal.

I went back upstairs and got into my pajamas again, but I was too wound up to sleep, so I fired up my laptop and did some digging. Spider was happy to settle in beside me on the couch. Maybe he needed to sleep off the nip.

There was nothing of note about Toly, just an old mention in the Tombstone, the local paper, about welcoming the new Santa's Workshop manager. It didn't surprise me. Most elves, but especially those in the North Pole, had zero online presence. Besides electronics only working sporadically in the NP, we just didn't do social media.

I Googled the missing employees next. Same

result. Nothing except for two more mentions in the Tombstone. The first was a photo from a charity function, and the other was about one of them, Franny Isler, participating in a fun run. No surprise there, considering I'd seen her, or a woman I thought was her, in the park out for a jog.

I stared at the screen, bathed in the blue glow, and thought about all the unanswered questions in my head. Didn't take long for me to type in a new search request.

Google took me to the home page for Star Brite Cleaners. The business had been established in 2009 and listed an address in a town I didn't recognize. A map search showed me that town was right outside of Nocturne Falls. Close enough to be local. I browsed through the site but found nothing that might explain why Toly had stopped using them.

Even their online reviews were good.

I typed in Thrifty Maids next. No website, but there was a Facebook page with only a handful of likes and a smattering of posts that were all a couple years old. I poked around without finding much. The owner of the company was listed as Elena Frye. A search on that name turned up nothing.

Why had Toly switched to this company? I held on to my belief that they had to be cheaper, but were they any good? They had no online reviews.

"Spider, this is a lost cause." I glanced down at him. He was passed out cold and snoring softly. "I'm glad it's not keeping you awake, though."

I shut my laptop, picked him up and carried him to bed. As I lay there, whipsawed by trying to figure out what was going on, I finally gave up and shifted my thoughts to Greyson.

And Cooper.

And how very different life was when I wasn't Jayne Frost.

Dr Pepper was really the only thing keeping me upright behind the counter the next morning. I hated that I was such a slug because Juniper had to pick up my slack, but these late-night investigations were putting a serious freeze on my beauty sleep. Something I needed desperately.

It didn't help that Toly had been in and out all day, back and forth between his office and the store. After the massive sales of Snowy Saturday, he was all fired up about getting inventory done and making a list so we could restock.

That would be fun. Ugh. I knew it needed doing, but I'd have rather just spent the day behind the counter with Juniper, chatting up the customers and helping the ones who needed it. Restocking was *actual* work. I yawned for like the fiftieth time. Loudly.

Juniper looked over from changing the register

paper and shook her head. "How late were you out with Count Chocula?"

"Almost eleven." But it had been after one in the morning by the time I'd actually gotten into bed.

"So?" she prodded. "How was your date?"

I smiled. How could I not? "Good. Really good. We went to this great little French restaurant and ate the best food and talked about nothing and everything, and it was perfect." Oh boy. I definitely sounded infatuated.

Her eyes went all twinkly. "Really? Perfect? Does that mean he kissed you?"

"Yes, and you know what else?" I waggled my head side to side. "I kissed him right back."

She let out a high-pitched noise and clapped her hand over her mouth. Thankfully, the only customers in the store were in the back and probably hadn't heard her over the Christmas music. "What was it like?"

"Oh, you know…" As good as kissing Cooper had been once upon a time, before he'd decided he couldn't handle *us*. Maybe better. My grin might have become permanently affixed. "Amazing."

Her eyes went from twinkly to shocked. "Could you feel his fangs? Did he try to bite you? You didn't let him, did you?"

"No, no and no. I get the sense that a vampire doesn't bite someone casually." Or at least Greyson didn't.

"Good." She seemed relieved.

I laughed. "Why? You think he's going to try to sway me to the dark side?"

She swatted my arm. "Don't even say things like that. Besides, I don't think we can be turned, seeing as how we're already supernaturals."

"I have no idea." And I doubted I'd ever find out. At some point, I'd be back in the NP and Greyson would be taking some other lucky woman to Café Claude. I sighed. What a depressing thought.

I was about to go check on the customers in an attempt to keep myself awake, when a woman I didn't recognize stuck her head through the warehouse door. "Excuse me, have you seen Toly?"

Juniper leaned to look past me. "He's in the remote-controlled vehicles sections doing inventory."

"Thanks, Juniper." The woman walked into the store and made a beeline for the area Juniper had mentioned. She had the tall, slender physique of most elves and the traditional, elegant good looks, including the bright white hair of someone with significant power.

As she disappeared into the back, I nudged Juniper. "Who is that?"

"That's Cookie. Toly's granddaughter."

Interesting. "She has a key to the warehouse?"

Juniper's mouth bunched to one side. "Huh. I never really thought about it, but she must."

"How else would she have come through the back door?"

"Right. Well, she is Toly's granddaughter."

"I guess that puts her on the permanently approved list." Made sense, her being family and all. "She's the one that owns the bed and breakfast?"

Juniper nodded. "Yep. When she was going through the divorce and the place was in trouble, she was here a lot more. But I guess things have picked back up."

"What makes you say that?"

She shrugged. "She only stops by once a week now. If that."

"I'm sure she needed someone to talk to during the divorce."

Juniper's expression was filled with compassion. "Oh, yeah. It was pretty awful. She thought she was going to lose the B&B in the settlement. She even had to take a second job for a while."

"The threat of losing her home and business must have been super stressful. But I guess she could have come to work here if it had actually happened."

"Probably. But…it wouldn't be the same."

"Not at all." Made me think that leaving Cooper and Greyson behind might not be such a bad thing.

It was scary to me how relationships could go so wrong. My parents were a great example of the opposite of that, as were my uncle Kris and aunt Martha. But there was no guarantee I'd end up that well-matched.

Cooper had already proven that once. I wasn't keen on giving him a chance to do it again. Greyson, however...I might be willing to let him break my heart a little.

Half an hour later, Toly presented me with the restocking list, and my time for mulling things over was gone. By the time five o'clock rolled around and Buttercup and Owen rolled in to relieve us, I was done.

Like, in need of a nap done. But I couldn't nap, because as I walked into my apartment, my thoughts returned in full force.

I had work to do. I got a hold of my dad on the snow globe. He was at the dinner table. I gave him props for keeping that snow globe with him all the time. It felt like a warm hug to know he was that concerned about staying in contact with me. "Hi, Dad. Sorry to interrupt your dinner."

"Don't worry about it, sweetheart." He wiped his mouth and set his napkin aside. "What's going on?"

"First of all, what did Mom make?"

"Chicken pot pie."

I groaned with jealousy. I could practically smell

it and taste the flaky pastry she used. "I love her chicken pot pie."

He smiled. "I probably shouldn't tell you she made French silk pie for dessert."

I clutched my heart. "You're killing me."

My mom stuck her head next to my dad's. "Hi, honey. I'll make you this dinner when you get home."

"Now I really want to get this thing solved."

My mom waved and disappeared as my dad's brows pulled together. "Are you closer?"

Maybe, but I wasn't ready to share my speculations just yet. "I'm working on it."

"What can I do to help?"

"Any chance you could get me the file on Toly's granddaughter?"

He pushed back in his chair. "I'll go to the records room right now."

"No, no. Sit down and eat. It's not that important. This isn't even a hunch. I just want to know more about her in hopes of learning more about Toly."

He sat. "You're sure?"

"Yes. Mom's chicken pot pie versus the endless, dusty pit of the records room? No contest. Plus, I could use a nap."

"All right. I'll go as soon as I'm done. Give me an hour. Two, tops."

"Good enough. Thanks."

"You're welcome. Love you."

"Love you too." I pressed the button and ended the conversation. A two-hour nap sounded blissful.

I was halfway to the bedroom when someone knocked on my door. I opened it, and Juniper smiled at me.

"Hey, you want to hang out and get some pizza? I'd ask if you want to go to Howler's, but based on how many times you yawned today, I thought you'd rather stay in."

I'd rather be in bed, but I could sleep anytime. My days here were limited. "That would be great."

"Good, because I already ordered two pies from Salvatore's. A king and an extra cheese. Cool?"

"Nicely done. You would be the perfect wife."

She laughed. "They're about half an hour out, so come over when you're ready."

"I'm going to change into something more lounge-y, feed Spider, then I'm there."

"Okay. See you then."

I shut the door and called my dad right back. "Hey, I'm going across the hall to eat pizza with a friend. Take your time on that file."

He smiled like he was pleased to hear I'd made a friend. For a moment, I felt about eight years old. "You got it. Have fun."

I shut the globe down and went to change. Once I was in my yoga pants and a big sweatshirt, I fed

Spider, grabbed a couple of Dr Peppers, stuck some cash in my bra, and locked up.

Juniper answered her door right away. "Hey, come on in."

"Wow, your place is so much...homier than mine." Colorful art decorated the walls, while more color adorned her couch in pillows and throws. She'd added area rugs and little knick-knacks and a bright tablecloth on the kitchen table.

My apartment looked like a hotel room. Hers looked like a home.

She shrugged. "I've been here longer. You tend to accumulate stuff."

"This is more than accumulating stuff. It's really nice."

"Thanks. I got most of this stuff at garage sales."

"Seriously?"

She nodded, smiling. "You'd be amazed at what you can find. I'd be happy to take you." Her smile vanished. "Except that since we're down a worker, the chances of both of us getting a Saturday off together are pretty slim. We can still go, but you'd have to get up early. Like six a.m."

"Ouch."

She laughed. "You're not an early riser, are you?"

Not when I spent my evenings trying to find out where the employees were disappearing to. "I can be. If properly motivated."

"Good to know. Hey, you want to watch a movie? That new Tom Hardy movie just hit On Demand. You know the one where he's a genie who ends up falling for the woman who finds his bottle on the beach?"

"You mean that gender-swapped *I Dream of Jeannie* remake? Oh, I'm down for that. *I Dream of Jimmy* it is." I made myself at home on the couch and twisted the top off one of my Dr Peppers. "Thanks for inviting me over, by the way."

"No problem. I'm happy to have the company." She grabbed a Coke for herself out of the fridge, then joined me on the couch and turned on the TV to find the movie.

The opening credits were rolling when someone knocked on her door. She hit pause and jumped up. "Pizza's here!"

I dug into my bra for a twenty. "Here."

She took it. "I'll have change for you in a sec." She paid the guy, took the pizzas and we were chowing down to the visual delights of Tom Hardy in harem pants in no time flat.

I was about to reach for my third slice when a thought occurred to me. I picked up the remote and hit pause instead. I looked at Juniper. "The pizza guy came right to your door."

"Mm-hmm," Juniper answered around a bite of king pie.

"So he's on the approved list?"

"Yep." She washed it down with a slug of Coke.

"How many people are on the approved list?"

She shrugged. "I have no idea."

I hit play and took my third slice in hand. Looked like I had another trip to Toly's office in my future.

I got back to my apartment around nine, filled with pizza and thoroughly entertained by the handsome Mr. Hardy and Juniper's stellar companionship. I also found myself a little saddened again, knowing that this was just a temporary situation.

Which sucked. I liked this life. Working at the store was actually pretty fun when Toly wasn't adding tasks to our to-do lists. Shocking, I know, but dealing with humans wasn't the nightmare I'd anticipated. For the most part, they were really nice. Most of them were so jazzed about being in a place like Nocturne Falls that their happiness was borderline contagious. And putting the right toy into the hands of a child was magical. I could see what drove my uncle Kris. And why elves wanted to work at the stores. It was a good life.

But the best part of this whole adventure was

having a friend like Juniper. That was something I'd never really expected. Or experienced. Not even with Lark. Juniper was so undemanding. What you saw was what you got with Juniper. And what you got was good.

I felt like I was on a vacation from my real life and I didn't want it to end.

But the snow in the globe was spinning, and my next moves were just ahead of me, bringing me closer to the end of this surprisingly fun trip.

"Hey, Dad."

"Hi. How was your pizza?"

"Great. We watched a movie and hung out. It was a really nice evening."

"I'm glad to hear it. I have some bad news. Well, no news, actually. There's no file on Toly's granddaughter."

"Then she never lived in the North Pole?"

"Never. Toly's son never returned to the NP after college. And so his daughter, Toly's granddaughter, has always lived in the human world."

Interesting. Elves that never spent time in the North Pole tended to have very different perspectives on things. "If Toly's son is her father, her last name would be Featherstone too." I was assuming that she'd gone back to her maiden name after such a bad divorce.

My dad nodded. "Should be. Why? What aren't you telling me?"

"Nothing, really. Just thinking out loud." I yawned without meaning to. "Sorry about that."

He smiled. "Get some sleep, sweetheart."

"I will. Thanks for the info."

"You're welcome. Sorry I couldn't help more."

We hung up. A minute later, I was on my laptop plugging Cookie Featherstone and bed & breakfast into the search bar.

At last Google gave me something I could use. Her B&B was called the Gingerbread Inn, and according to the website, it was currently booked for the next couple of months. No vacancy was a good sign, so Juniper was right. The place must be doing okay.

I still wanted to see it for myself. Thankfully, tomorrow was my day off. I could sleep in a little *and* make some headway on my mission. Hopefully. I stretched, tired and ready for bed. I needed to visit Toly's office again to see if I could find that list of approved visitors, but I couldn't risk it until the store was closed and I was sure he'd turned in.

That meant at least eleven o'clock. Ugh. I didn't think I could keep my eyes open that long. I compromised and set my phone alarm for midnight.

I was in bed and asleep five minutes later.

By twelve thirty-six, I'd hit the snooze four times. I finally made myself sit up. Groggy was an understatement. Fortunately, I'd slept in my black yoga pants and a black T-shirt to make my life easier. Go, me!

I put on my boots and my black hoodie, grabbed my keys and my phone and went downstairs for a little breaking and entering.

Toly's office was messier than I remembered. Who could find anything in this clutter? I sat in his desk chair and started going through his drawers, which thankfully weren't locked. Lots of files in the first one, but none marked Visitor List or anything like that. In fact, none of the labels made much sense at all.

I brought my phone a little closer to shine more light on the files and tried to blink the sleepiness out of my brain. What on earth was Super Fun Snaps and Lobberball?

I pulled a file and opened it and understood immediately. These were toy designs. Stuff he was actively working on, based on the dates next to the notes.

That made sense given the mock-ups on his shelves and the pieces and parts littering every square inch of his desk.

I wondered if he'd submitted any of them to the company, but since I'd never seen any of them on the shelves, I guessed not.

I propped my elbows on his desk and rested my head in my hands. This wasn't getting me any closer to finding the list of approved visitors. And if the pizza guy was approved, Jack the Ripper could probably get in. Not that pizza guys were dangerous. To the contrary. They were right up there with tooth fairies and my uncle.

I sighed. The missing employees could have been abducted, for all I knew. Except for Franny Isler, who I was sure I'd seen living as a human. I was also sure I hadn't seen an elven bracelet on her.

So what did that mean?

I had no freaking idea.

The elevator chimed, and like the other night, the sound put me into a state of temporary panic. I shoved everything back into its proper place and hurried around the desk to see what I could through the pebbled glass window.

Just like last time, it wasn't the apartment elevator. Two forms stood silhouetted by the light coming out of the restricted elevator. One reminded me of the tall, slim figure I'd seen leaving before. That one looked like they had their hand on the shoulder of the second, shorter figure.

The pair stepped onto the elevator. It seemed as if the taller one was guiding the shorter one in, but then again, I was looking through pebbled glass and then another clear glass window in the vestibule doors. The elevator closed and they were gone.

I started back toward Toly's desk. Nocturne

Falls employees weren't my business. Then a creeping suspicion stopped me, and I knew if I didn't act on it, I'd always wonder.

I slipped out of the office, took a few moments against the door to let my head come right. I knew just standing there that my gut had been dead on, but I walked over to the vestibule anyway, pushed through the vestibule doors and sniffed.

Unless there was a Nocturne Falls employee who wore the same old-man aftershave as Owen, he'd been the short one getting on the elevator.

Sleeping in would have been nice, but I woke up early, determined to make serious headway into why all those employees had quit and disappeared. How was I going to make this headway? Let's just say I had a massive amount of next-level snooping to do.

Starting with the Gingerbread Inn.

The employees had begun leaving around the same time that Toly's granddaughter's divorce had happened. I believed it was very possible that the stress Toly had dealt with on her behalf had changed him. Maybe caused him to have bouts of moodiness that had scared off the employees. And despite Juniper telling me the inn was doing better, I wanted to see for myself.

The morning was cool and a little drizzly, but the gray weather suited me just fine. I pulled together the sort of outfit I hoped I disappeared in: black yoga pants, my hooded black sweatshirt and black running shoes.

Being noticed while snooping wasn't my goal.

I stuck my phone, my keys and a twenty in my pocket, but no ID. Just in case. I had another gambit I could put into play too, but not just yet. And only if I really needed to. Removing my bracelet.

I left the bikes behind in favor of walking, but I did grab an umbrella from the stand. That felt more inconspicuous than riding a bike in the drizzle. Plus, the umbrella gave me something to hide under. And if I had to, I could ditch it without feeling bad.

Twenty minutes later, I stopped under a tree to check the nav on my phone. The rain had petered out, but it was still gray and gloomy. Two and a half blocks to go. I memorized the route, going with one that would take me around the property, and left the umbrella propped by the tree.

When I got to the street, I slowed considerably. It was a cute house, sort of a modern Victorian that had extra gingerbread added to it to really sell the name. Even the colors, a toasty brown with trim in white, yellow and bright blue, made it look like its namesake. I could see why it would be popular.

A man in a khaki jumpsuit was working in the yard. I wouldn't have thought a gardener would pick a day like today to tend to his plants, but summer was right around the corner, and what did I know about that kind of stuff?

He hauled a wheelbarrow full of trimmings to the curb, coming right past me. He looked at me and smiled. "Morning."

"Morning." I stared at him, my stomach clenching hard. I knew that face. Sure, the hair color was different, and his ears weren't pointed, but the man in front of me was as familiar as family at this point. "Will?"

His smile held without the slightest waver. "Sorry, ma'am. I'm Travis."

Like hell he was. I checked his wrists, thankful his sleeves were pushed up. He wasn't wearing an elven bracelet. "My apologies. You look like someone I know."

He nodded. "I get that sometimes. Have a good—"

"Have you worked here long? I have friends coming into town, and I was wondering if it's a nice place."

"Oh, sure, real nice place. But I don't think there are any vacancies for a while. Lots of repeat customers."

I pressed him again. "You sound like you've been here awhile."

His gaze shifted, like he was trying to recall. "Almost three years, I guess."

Which was about how long ago he'd left Santa's Workshop. "And you like it? The owner is nice?"

"Yep. Ms. Frye—sorry, Featherstone, I always get that wrong, I mean, I know she's divorced and all—anyway, she's real good people."

Frye? The name punched me in the gut. "Thanks. I appreciate that. You have a good day."

"You too." He went back to work.

In a haze of thought, I walked to the next block and found a trolley bench to sit on. What were the chances that Cookie's given name was Elena and she was the Elena Frye who owned Thrifty Maids? At the very least, they had to be related. This wasn't that big of a town. Either way, add in that one of the store's former employees was now working at the Gingerbread Inn and looking as human as Franny Isler, and something seriously stank.

I had to get into the Gingerbread Inn and look around. Who cared if there was no vacancy? It was a business. Anyone could go in and inquire.

What they did after they got inside, well, that was where I'd deviate. So long as I had the chance.

But I couldn't risk Cookie recognizing me as one of the store's employees. After all, she'd walked right by me yesterday. There was no way she hadn't seen me. Fortunately, my father had already told me she'd never spent a day in the NP in her life.

Her loss, my gain. I tugged the sleeve of my hoody back and took off the silver bracelet masking my appearance. I felt the magic leaving me like a cool breeze zipping past. I checked myself in the reflection of my phone's dark screen.

Yep, Jayne Frost again. It was nice to see my real face after a week of being Lilibeth. Weird, but nice.

I took a breath and tried to make a plan, but really how could I until I got inside and knew what sort of opportunity I was going to have?

My heart raced as I walked back to the inn. Will was gone out of the front yard. That was good. I hustled up the steps and went inside.

The place was surprisingly quiet for a B&B at full occupancy. Especially on a rainy day when the weather didn't make walking around or sightseeing high on most people's lists. Not a soul in sight, but I could hear a television. Barely. It was turned down low. If someone was watching it, they had excellent hearing.

Just inside the door was a small front desk. A tarnished brass bell sat on the desk, but I wasn't about to ring it.

Beside the bell, the desk held a registry, and on the wall behind it were pegs with numbers over top of them. For room keys, most likely. Except there were no keys. That supported the full occupancy, but where was everyone? In their rooms? That sounded boring. And unlikely.

A hall led back from the foyer and there was a door at the end, but I started with the first room I came to, sticking my head in. It was a lounge. The TV that I'd heard was in there, playing a daytime game show. The lack of volume apparently didn't matter, because the room was empty.

The room on the other side of the hall was a dining room. A coffee and tea service was set up on the buffet. I snuck in and put my hand on the carafe. It was warm like it still had coffee in it. Maybe breakfast had been served, but there wasn't an aroma of food in the air.

A swinging door adjoined the dining room to another. I put my ear to it and heard nothing. I pushed it open slightly and peeked in. The kitchen. Also empty. A few bowls and side plates sat drying on a dish rack along with a handful of silverware. Not exactly the aftermath of dishes I would have expected for a B&B at full occupancy. I mean, it was called a bed and *breakfast* for a reason, right?

Maybe Cookie skimped on that part. Maybe she just did continental and only put out coffee and pastries and a little cold cereal. But for a place with no vacancy and repeat visitors, you'd think there'd be a big spread.

I went into the kitchen cautiously, governing the door behind me as it closed so as not to make any extra noise. Through the window over the sink, the backyard was visible beyond a screened porch. I could just make out the edge of a large shed. That might be where Will had gone.

There were three more doors in the kitchen. One that went out to the porch, one that seemed positioned to lead into the main part of the house and matched up with the door I'd seen at the end of the hall, and another, smaller door on the side. Could be a pantry. Or the cook's quarters?

But didn't the owner cook breakfast? Hmm. Maybe Cookie's room then. Which meant I really needed to get in there.

My heart didn't agree as my pulse sped up a notch. I blew out a breath, trying to calm myself. I'd gotten this far.

I tiptoed to the door and listened. Nothing. I tried the knob. Locked.

Now I wanted in more than ever.

I slipped in Saint Nick style.

I patted the wall until I found a light switch, then flipped it on. Even with my spinning head, I could tell the room was tiny, like an old pantry that had been turned into an office. There was a narrow built-in desk with a closed laptop on it and a few stacks of papers and files. Two wire shelves ran from wall to wall, and both held toy prototypes.

Did Toly work over here? That made no sense. Unless this was stuff he was doing outside of the company. That could be. Especially if he was trying to make extra money to help Cookie out.

I poked through the files. One was marked Orders To Be Filled, another said Customers, and a third was simply labeled Underweb. What the heck that was I had zero idea, but other than the Customers file, none of them made much sense. What orders did a B&B have to fill?

But Toly might. If he was selling his own toys. Wasn't that a conflict of interest? I grabbed a sheet of paper and held it up to the light.

Same watermark. Toly was definitely working here. And whatever he was doing, he didn't want anyone at the shop to know about it.

With my heart still pounding, I pulled out my phone, flipped through the paperwork, and snapped pics of anything that looked vaguely important. I'd figure out if any of it actually was when I got back to my apartment because all I wanted now was out of here.

The back door creaked open. I flipped the light off and froze. If that was Cookie and she was coming in here, I was trapped. There was no window, and no other way out.

Was this Jacque's vision of me in a dark room in danger? I held my breath and prayed that he might be wrong just once.

Feet stomped, like someone knocking dirt off their shoes. Then more footsteps, thankfully receding. Maybe Will coming in from the shed. Whoever it was, it didn't sound like they'd stayed in the kitchen.

Enough was enough. I was getting out while I could. I went back under the door and stumbled out through the screened porch. The rain was back. I pulled my hood up as I passed an old pickup parked in front of the shed. It bore the Gingerbread Inn name and phone number on the side, which was about the only spot not dented.

I kept going, crossing into the adjoining neighbor's property. If anyone saw me, they'd probably report me for public drunkenness. I knew I was weaving, but there was no time to rest and let the dizziness pass.

As soon as I was on the sidewalk, I slipped my

bracelet back on, happy to hide behind Lilibeth's face again.

It took a good ten minutes for my heartrate and my head to return to normal. I wasn't ready to go back to the apartment yet, though. The thought of being that close to Toly and whatever he was up to just didn't sit well with me. What I needed was to think and the thing that helped me think best was sugar.

My nav showed me the shortest route to Delaney's, where thankfully the rain had diminished the usual crowd. I ordered a fat slice of chocolate cake called Tall, Dark and Delicious and a Dr Pepper.

I collected my cake and my soda and took up residence at a corner table where I could have my back to the wall and still view the door and the street beyond. Sue me, I was feeling a little paranoid.

The first bite of that cake took the edge off. The chocolatey goodness kicked in some positive endorphins and helped mellow me out. I scrolled through the pictures I'd taken, trying to make sense of those files.

I still couldn't. And my brain was tired of trying. I texted Greyson.

Does underweb mean anything to you?

His response came faster than I'd anticipated. *No. Are you home?*

Nope. At Delaney's having cake.
Stay there.

Like I was going to leave Tall, Dark and Delicious for Tall, Dark and Suddenly Bossy. I was halfway through that cake and debating a second piece when he showed up. Vampire speed was pretty impressive.

He slipped into the other chair in a whirlwind of black leather, burgundy silk and gleaming silver. His brocade scarf would have looked ridiculous on anyone else, but on him it was rakish and sexy. More vampire magic, no doubt. He studied me. "How do you know about the underweb?"

He spoke in hushed tones, but there was only one other occupied table, and that was on the far side of the store. I frowned at him. This was not the greeting I'd expected. "Good morning to you too."

He blinked slowly, then smiled. "My apologies. Good morning, Lilibeth. How are you?"

I shrugged. "Better since this cake." I started to take another bite, then stopped and stared at him. "How are you here?"

"You texted."

"No, I mean, it's *day time*. Come to think of it, the sun wasn't completely set when I saw you on the street Friday. How do you do that? Doesn't the sun make you go boom?"

He rolled his eyes. "Vampires turn to ash in the sun, they do not explode."

"Excuse me for not knowing exactly how sunlight kills you." I shook my head. "You should not be here."

"It's fine. I have Roma magic that protects me."

"You're sure?"

He cocked an eyebrow. "You think I'd be here if I wasn't?"

"Point taken. Thanks for coming, by the way."

"You're welcome." He leaned in. "Now please, how do you know about the underweb?"

"I don't. That's why I asked you. And you sound like you know what it is, so why did you text me that you didn't know?"

He sighed. "It's not something worth involving yourself with."

Well, now my interest was really piqued. "I'm not involving myself with it. I just want to know what it is."

His eyes narrowed. "Why?"

What could I say? I wasn't about to confess my little B&E at the B&B. "I think it has something to do with the store employees who've left."

He snorted softly. "I wouldn't be surprised. Except that things like that don't happen in Nocturne Falls."

I groaned. His cloak-and-dagger answers weren't helping. "Can you please stop speaking in such vague terms? What is the underweb?"

"Keep your voice down, please." He glanced

around, but no one, including the woman behind the counter, was paying us any attention. As I took another forkful of cake, he leaned one elbow on the table and put his hand to his forehead for a moment. "The underweb is a shadowy, unsearchable corner of the Internet. It is devoted to the worst deviances of our kind."

I swallowed. "You mean supernatural things?"

"Yes. And it is best left alone."

I put my fork down. "What kinds of things are we talking about?"

"Transactions in black magic, pilfered magic, assassinations, slaves, unholy spells, sexual deviations of the supernatural variety, blood trade...any unsavory activity you can imagine can be found there. And those who dabble in the trade of the underweb tend to be criminals and miscreants. The very type this town strives to keep out."

"Wow."

He picked up my fork and helped himself to a bite of cake. "Wow indeed. How did you come to find out about it?"

"I could ask you the same question."

He nodded. "You could."

"And would you give me an answer?"

He stared at me a moment, then got up. "Excuse me."

I thought he was leaving, but he only went up to the counter to get some coffee.

He came back with it, sat down and stared at the oily black liquid steaming in his cup. His gaze seemed a million miles away, and disgust bracketed his mouth in harsh lines. "My last lover was a very wealthy woman."

My brows lifted. Sure, I knew logically I wasn't the first woman to catch Greyson's eye, but to hear him call another woman *lover* was sort of...odd. "How nice for you."

He shook his head and looked out the window. "Life was good. She was very generous, and while I have plenty of money of my own, she rarely let me spend it." He glanced back at me. "*Let me spend it* sounds wrong. I should say I rarely had the chance. She paid for everything and liked it that way."

I just nodded and let him go on.

"Europe was our playground. It's very different over there for vampires."

"She was one too?"

"Yes. Older. A little more powerful. Well educated. But she didn't have my street smarts." A wry smile bent his mouth. "We made a good team."

"And you loved her?"

He hesitated. "Maybe. At least I thought I did. She was certainly entertaining."

"So what happened?"

His smile disappeared. "About a year ago, she started supplying us with exotic blood."

"What does that mean exactly?"

He traced a pattern on the table. "Supernatural blood. Shifters, witches, fae...blood that contained more power than ordinary human blood."

"And that wasn't good?" What did I know about vampires and blood and all that business?

He rolled his shoulders like they'd suddenly tensed up. "No. It's an unwritten rule that drinking from another supernatural without their permission is off-limits. In fact, the vampire council maintains that drinking from anyone against their will is forbidden."

You learn something new every day.

"Because of that I was curious about her source. She wouldn't tell me, just insisted it was all on the up and up. That wasn't enough for me. I did some digging and found out she was getting the blood from a supplier via the underweb. At that point, I didn't know what it was either."

I leaned in. "So how did you find out?"

He put his hands around his cup. "A lot of trial and error and subterfuge. But I finally gained access to the underweb, and after about two months of poking around and pretending to be someone I wasn't in that dark, disgusting corner, I uncovered her supplier. He wasn't getting the blood voluntarily. I left her immediately."

"Good for you. Was she angry?" I would think losing a man like Greyson would ruin any woman's day.

His smile was bitter. "I don't know. I didn't stay to find out. Just wrote her a note telling her what I knew and left."

Just like the store employees. "And now you're here."

"And now I'm here. And you know my secret."

"That was a secret?"

"You're the first person I've told."

Things suddenly felt very unbalanced. I bit my lip and tried to ignore that feeling. I failed, but I tried. "I appreciate your trust in me." Something he'd now demonstrated twice. I tapped my fingers on the table. "Can you still access the underweb?"

"Yes. But I have no plans to ever again. The place is a sewer."

"What if I needed some help?"

He peered at me with great suspicion. "What are you up to, Lilibeth? Are you in some kind of trouble?"

"No. Not yet anyway." I took a breath. "I don't want to go into it here. And I don't think my apartment is the right place either."

"Because I'm not on the approved list or another reason?"

"Another reason." I wanted to be on neutral ground when I revealed who I really was, so going to his place didn't seem like a good idea. "Do you know somewhere more private we could go to talk? Somewhere close?"

He thought for a moment, then nodded. "Follow me."

We ended up at Café Claude, which wasn't open yet. Jacque was in the back prepping food, and after Greyson had a word with him, he promised we wouldn't be disturbed.

Greyson stood before me, arms crossed. The restaurant was dark and we were a little distance from the front windows, but even in the watery light of the outside gloom he looked so handsome my eyes hurt. "Tell me what's going on."

I was nervous and rightly so, but this was definitely a rip-the-bandage-off-quickly kind of situation. I put my hand on my bracelet. "I'm not Lilibeth Holiday."

His brows lifted slightly. "Then who are you?"

I pulled the bracelet off. "I'm Jayne Frost, daughter of the Winter King."

Greyson's eyes widened briefly. Then he stared at me a long, hard second. "As in Jack Frost, the Winter King? Which makes you…"

"The Winter Princess."

He nodded slowly. "Go on."

His expression was so hard to read I couldn't be sure what he was thinking. "I'm here to find out what's happened to our last six employees, and I could use your help."

At last, his eyes lit with amusement, and he

sketched a bow. "I had no idea I was dating a princess. I am at your service, my lady."

"Yeah, yeah, very cute."

He smirked. "I take it you don't think the other employees would be straight with you if you showed up as their princess."

"Right. Because I tend to get two kinds of reactions. People either avoid me like the plague or treat me with such false kindness that I can never get a read on their true intentions."

He considered that. "Thank you for confiding in me. I will try not to treat you any differently."

"Thanks." That was sweet of him to say, but it didn't do much to allay the sadness I was already feeling. I knew it would change what was between us. That's how life worked when you were elven royalty.

He pulled out a chair for me at the nearest table. "What can I do to help?"

I sat, and he joined me as I explained what I'd found in Cookie's office. "Now that you've told me what the underweb is, the files marked Orders To Be Filled make a lot more sense."

He nodded. "So Toly's selling something. Makes sense he'd do it from her place."

"Well, he can't do it from his office. The stores don't use the Internet. A touch-screen register system is as techie as we get. And if he logged on from his apartment, and he was using the company-provided Wi-Fi, there'd be a record of his activities, right?"

"Right. So what is he selling?"

"That's what I was hoping you could help me find out."

"I'll do my best, but it could take a while. The underweb is built on shadows. No one uses their real name or location. Everything is hidden within layers and layers of secrecy."

"Makes sense, considering. I guess whatever he's up to, it can't be good, can it?"

"Not if the underweb is his market of choice."

I sighed. "I'd thought maybe he was selling toy designs outside of the company, but he wouldn't need the underweb for that."

Greyson shrugged. "Maybe. Maybe not. Depends on the toys."

"That's an unpleasant thought."

"I'll see what I can find out."

"Thank you." I bounced the bracelet on my knee. "Please don't say a word to anyone about who I really am."

"I won't."

"I'm sorry I lied to you. I thought you'd figured me out when you touched my bracelet that night in Insomnia."

"I guess I had, but your explanation seemed plausible." He smiled. "You're pretty quick on your feet. I can see why you were sent to figure this out." Then he squinted slightly. "You're far more powerful than you let on, aren't you?"

I nodded. "Yes. Another of my secrets that must be kept."

He canted his head, taking me in. "I'm going to assume you don't really want an interview with the Ellinghams, either."

"Not really an interview, but I wouldn't mind talking to them to see if they know more about the missing employees than they've told my father. At this point, if anyone's poaching workers, my best guess would be Cookie Featherstone, Toly's granddaughter. And if she is doing it, maybe Toly is somehow wiping their memories." I sighed. "I really don't know what to think right now, but talking to the Ellinghams might give me some new info in case my supposition about Toly turns out to be a dead end."

He frowned. "You think the Ellinghams might be holding something back? I doubt that very highly, especially when the safety of supernaturals is at issue. That's the whole reason this town was created; to give our kind a safe haven. I just can't imagine they'd do that. Not when it could damage the town's reputation."

"They're not very forthcoming about the Basement."

"Protecting town secrets isn't the same thing at all."

I considered that. "You're sure they're not holding anything back?"

"I'd stake my immortality on it."

"All right. I believe you. Just like I believe you aren't going to tell anyone about me, right?"

He lifted my hand and kissed my knuckles. "I won't tell a soul. Now put that bracelet back on before someone sees you."

I did, then glanced at him. He was studying me. "What?"

"Lilibeth is very pretty. But the real you has something she doesn't."

"What?"

He shook his head slowly. "It's not something I can name, but it's good. A quality of genuineness that shines through."

"Does that mean you like the real me better?"

"How could I not?" His eyes gleamed bright silver, and a mischievous smile caused his mouth to twitch. "Your Highness."

The sun showed its face when I was about two blocks from the apartment. The day had turned out pretty well. And with Greyson looking into Toly's underweb dealings, I finally felt like I was getting somewhere.

It was almost one o'clock, and despite having cake, I was hungry. I know, shocking, right? I thought maybe I'd run over to Howler's and have some lunch instead of scrounging something up at the apartment. Then I remembered what I was wearing.

I really needed to change out of my criminal clothes first. Plus they were damp from walking in the rain.

Then my phone almost vibrated out of my pocket. I pulled it out to check what was going on but couldn't read the texts in the bright sun. I doubted Greyson had found anything yet, but who knew? I put the hustle on it and got back to the warehouse as fast as I could.

As soon as I was through the vestibule, I tapped the elevator button and pulled my phone out again. The messages were from Juniper, Buttercup and Toly.

Oh boy. Something was going on.

The elevator opened, and I got on. Then I started scrolling through Juniper's texts. I stared at my phone, unable to process what I was reading.

Owen was gone. As in *left a note and was never coming back to work again* gone.

That made seven.

I staggered out of the elevator and leaned against the wall to read the rest of the messages. Buttercup's were the same as Juniper's.

Toly was asking to see me right away due to a change in the schedule. Huh. You think? He was so cavalier about it. Had he gotten that used to employees leaving, or was he keeping things calm because he was responsible?

I let myself into my apartment and locked the door behind me. How could Owen be gone? I'd just seen and smelled him last night. At least I thought I had. Just like I thought whoever had been with him had been guiding him. I shivered at the thought that Owen might not have been in total control of himself.

I needed to get downstairs and talk to Juniper.

Toly, too, but he could wait. I wanted to be a little calmer when I spoke to him. Right now, my gut feeling was that he was an integral part of this. I had no idea what his connection was to the person with Owen and whatever was happening in the Basement, but my first reaction was to grab him and give him a good shake until he told me what was really going on.

Since I doubted that would go over well, I definitely needed to avoid him until I chilled a bit.

I fed Spider, then changed into something a little less ninja-esque and went downstairs. The light was on in Toly's office, so I assumed he was in there.

I kept going, into the store. Juniper had a hollow-eyed look about her, and Buttercup's eyes were red like she'd been crying. "Hey, guys, I just got your texts. I can't believe it."

Juniper nodded. "He's gone. Just like the others. Left a note and…" She shrugged.

Buttercup scowled. "He wouldn't do that."

"Leave a note?" I asked.

"No. *Leave*." She sniffed hard.

"How did you guys find out?"

Juniper sighed. "He didn't show for work. He was supposed to be on the overlap shift with Buttercup, but by twelve ten, he still hadn't shown. *Really* unlike him."

"Yeah," Buttercup said. "I told Toly so he went

up and checked Owen's apartment and found the note."

"What did the note say?"

"We don't know." Juniper looked at Buttercup before looking at me again. "Toly just said Owen claimed he'd met someone and was leaving with her."

The tall slim figure I'd seen Owen with definitely could have been female. "Um…that might be true."

They both looked at me, waiting for an explanation.

Granted, I hadn't seen them leave the warehouse together, but anything was possible. And if he had left with someone, he'd had to *want* to leave. Toly's management style was as good a reason as any for Owen to feel that way. "I told you I saw him the other night headed out on a date. And I think I might have seen him last night with someone."

Their eyes widened. "Who was it?"

"I don't know." And frankly, I hadn't thought it was a woman at the time.

"No way." Buttercup crossed her arms. "I'm telling you, the guy hardly ever left his apartment. He lived to game." She frowned. "Maybe he met someone online."

"Could be," Juniper said. "I hear that happens a lot."

I liked them thinking this way. It felt safer to me. At least until I knew more. "That's probably what happened." I hooked my thumb back toward the warehouse door. "I'm supposed to go talk to Toly about a change in the schedule. But I can come back after that."

Juniper smiled limply. "Lilibeth, it's your day off. Go enjoy it. There's nothing you can do anyway. Nothing any of us can do. Trust me. This is the fifth time an employee has skipped out since I've been here. We'll get through it."

"I know, but—"

"She's right," Buttercup said. "Take today while you can because until we get a replacement for him, there won't be any more days off for anyone."

"Okay, but let's get together tonight. Just the three of us. My place. I'll order Salvatore's pizza. My treat. Cool?"

They both nodded. "Cool."

I waved and went to face Toly, hoping I could keep from throttling him. I knocked on his office door. "Toly? It's Lilibeth."

"Come in, come in."

I opened the door. The mess I'd seen by the light of my phone was nothing compared to seeing it in all its well-lit glory. "Wow, you keep a lot of stuff in here."

"Hmm?" He looked around, blinking behind his glasses. "Oh yes, yes, I suppose I do."

That whole scattered tinker-brain thing wasn't playing with me right now. I took a deep breath and remembered this was not the time to start questioning him about his part in the elves going missing.

There was nowhere to sit, so I leaned against the filing cabinet. The same one I'd broken into twice. "I hear Owen went the way of his predecessors."

"Yes. Sad, isn't it?" Toly shook his head and sighed. It was Oscar-worthy. "He was a good worker. Sorry to see him go."

"Did he say anything to you?"

"No, just left a note."

"Can I see it?" Actually, I could already see it. Sitting front and center on his desk. Written on what looked like the same paper as the others.

That gave Toly a moment of pause. "I don't know if that would be proper—"

"Has anyone compared the notes he and the other workers left? I mean, you have to admit that it's pretty suspicious how this keeps happening."

"That's not your concern."

"Um, it is totally my concern. I'm an elf, and I work here. If something bad is happening, I don't want to be the next victim. Or do you think maybe they're all leaving so suddenly because they don't like working for you?"

Toly tugged at his apron and sat down, looking

as angry as a flea-infested yeti. "What is that supposed to mean?"

"Let's be honest, here. You're not exactly boss of the year. You don't give us decent breaks, you make us run the Snowy Saturdays when it's really your job, and you overload us with petty chores."

"I'm the manager. I make the rules. If you don't like it—"

"What? I can quit?" I leaned in. "Hand over my keys and leave all my stuff behind?"

Toly jumped to his feet. "Now see here."

"Oh, so *now* you're upset. But not about how many of your workers have left under odd circumstances. What if someone bad is targeting your employees? Do you even care?" I didn't wait for an answer, just straightened and held out my hand. "I'll take that new schedule and leave you alone so you can give that some thought."

His jaw dropped, but a second later he put the new schedule in my hand. Maybe I'd scared him. Or intimidated him. I was told I had that quality at times, but I wasn't sure it had transferred to Lilibeth.

I reached for the door knob, then stopped. "One more thing. You can put Greyson Garrett on your approved visitors list. He's going to be coming to see me." I smiled. "Just thought you should know."

"He-he's a vampire."

I tilted my head. "Is he? I thought he just had an

overbite." I sailed out and slammed the door behind me.

I shook with anger all the way back to my apartment. Toly was going down. I fired up my laptop and was about to run a few searches when someone knocked on my door.

If Toly thought he was going to fire me, he was so wrong it was painful. I yanked the door open, "Listen here—"

Cooper's brows shot up. "Bad time?"

I slowed my roll. "I thought you were someone else."

He grinned. "That's good. I'm glad I'm not that other person. You sound mad."

I leaned against the door jamb. "I was, but not at you." Who could be mad at Cooper in his fireman's uniform? Technically, I'm sure I could manage it, but right now I was happy to forget the past and enjoy this momentary distraction of eye candy. "So what's up?"

He lifted one muscled shoulder in a pretense of indifference. "I was in the neighborhood. Thought I'd see if you wanted to grab some lunch with me."

His timing was pretty good, but I had work to do. Although I might be able to think better if I calmed down. And what situation did food not make better? Because I was hungry. Still, I needed a little more convincing if I was going to take a break from figuring out this mess. I crossed my arms. "Where did you want to go?"

"How about pizza at Salvatore's?"

"As good as that pizza is, I'm having that tonight."

"Burgers at Howler's?" He waggled his brows. "We could split a peach cobbler."

"Sold." This would give me a chance to talk some things out with him, maybe get another perspective. And lunch out with him would keep me from storming back into Toly's office and strangling him until his eyes bugged out of his fat tinker head. Which was good because being a princess wouldn't get me out of a murder charge. "Let me get my purse."

Howler's was busy—it was lunch after all—but we got right in. Cooper explained that since his boss, the chief, was Bridget's brother *and* Bridget was also dating a fireman, firemen got priority seating. It was good to know people.

We slid into our booth and immediately ordered drinks, burgers and cobbler to follow. Menus were for tourists.

Cooper seemed pretty pleased that I'd agreed to join him. "How's your day going? You seem a little frazzled."

I took a moment to gather my thoughts. There were far too many of them. "I don't even know where to start."

"The beginning?"

"I guess." Except I didn't really want to tell him about my descent into a life of crime. I had a hunch he'd frown on my decision to break into Cookie's office. "How about I hit the highlights? Or should I say the lowlights? Another employee left today."

His mouth gaped. "Really? Who?"

"Owen."

He seemed relieved it hadn't been Juniper or Buttercup. I knew the feeling. He made a noise of disgust. "What the hell is going on in that shop?"

I shook my head. "I wish I knew. I'm starting to think it's Toly. He's not easy to work for."

Cooper splayed his hands on the table. "Could be. What other theories do you have? Because I know you have them."

I rolled my eyes. "Can you blame me? I work there. I deserve to know what's going on."

"You're right. You absolutely do."

I sighed. "Well, I thought maybe the Ellinghams were poaching workers, but I don't think that now."

"Yeah, that's highly unlikely. That's just not their style. Anything else?"

"Not really. But something is very off. I know that much."

"Like what?"

Our drinks arrived, so I held off answering until the server left. I stripped the paper off my straw, stuck it in my Dr Pepper and took a long drink. So much better. "It feels like something...bad. But I can't tell you more than that because that's all I have. A feeling."

And Greyson working the underweb angle, but I'd lay good money Cooper didn't know anything about something that nefarious.

"Feelings are valid. You have to listen to that stuff."

"I am. But it's like trying to put a puzzle together in the dark with half the pieces missing."

He nodded and drank his water. "Anything I can help you with? Anything that doesn't involve the elevator you're not authorized to use?"

I laughed. If only he knew Greyson had already helped me out with that one. Of course, after seeing Owen head down to the Basement, I'd love another visit, but I knew Cooper wasn't going to be my tour guide for that trip. "You know anything about the Gingerbread Inn?"

He sat back, a curious look on his face. "Why?"

"Just wondering. I know it's owned by the store manager's granddaughter. A woman named Cookie Featherstone. You know her?"

His expression darkened. "Is this some kind of game?"

I put my hands up. "I honestly have no idea what you're talking about."

Some of that darkness went away. "You're not

asking me about her because you found out I dated her?"

Now my mouth gaped. "Uh, *no*. I had no idea. None." I stared at him. "Wow. I never would have guessed. I suppose Juniper knows."

He shook his head and looked a little sheepish. "No. Neither does Buttercup. I thought you'd talked to Elena, and she'd mentioned it—"

I bent forward as a familiar chill socked me in the gut again. "Who?" But I already knew.

"Elena. Cookie."

His answer confirmed my suspicions. I bit back a curse as he kept talking.

"I know everyone calls her that, but it felt weird calling a grown woman Cookie."

I rubbed my forehead, my mind racing. Cookie owned the cleaning company. No wonder Toly was using her services. He'd want to help his granddaughter out as much as he could. But why hadn't he notified the Financial Department of the change? Sure, that wasn't mandatory and he didn't need authorization to make the switch, but he was so by-the-book with everything else. Was it because he was using her to clean up after employees left? That implied guilt, didn't it?

Cooper nodded. "Yeah. Anyway, it's not like I'm the only guy from the station she's dated, but that was a long time ago."

"Got it. And your business is your business."

"Thanks. What did you want to know about the inn?"

"I don't know." I stared into the bubbles of my Dr Pepper. How did this all fit together? What was I missing? And why was Will working at the Gingerbread Inn but had no idea who he really was?

"Hey, you okay?"

I glanced up. "I'm not sure yet."

"You want to talk about it?"

I sort of did, especially because he knew the town so well, but I wasn't going to do it here. In fact, maybe I just needed to wait until Greyson was free again. Either way, I couldn't just sit here. I had to put everything I knew on paper and see if I could connect it in a way that gave me something more to go on. "Thanks for inviting me to lunch, but I have to leave."

Cooper, being Cooper, got our server to pack everything up to go, and as a result, we were back in my apartment and I was pacing the floor with a double bacon cheeseburger in one hand while I tried to think.

The cheeseburger may or may not have been helping, but there was no way I was putting down something this delicious. Except maybe to get some fries. (Which were good but not fried in duck fat good. That bar had been set.)

Cooper was at the dining table eating his burger like a sane person, while Spider sat in the chair next to him, patiently waiting for attention. Or a taste of the burger. It was hard to tell. Cooper waved a fry at me. "Why don't you join me at the table so we can eat like normal people and talk this out?"

"I can't sit. I'm too wound up. I'm full of energy that has no place to go."

He got a twinkle in his eyes I recognized.

I shook my head. "Calm down, charm school. Not that kind of energy."

He lifted his burger. "Worth a shot."

"I need to make sense of what I know."

"I can help with that." He pulled a pen out of his pocket, then smoothed his big hand over the takeout bag to flatten it. "We'll diagram it."

I stopped pacing and came to the table. "I have a notebook."

"This'll do."

"Okay. Where do we start?"

He held his pen above the bag. "Who do you know the most about?"

"Toly." I finished the last bite of my burger and went to the sink to wash my hands.

Cooper wrote his name down. "Tell me what you know about him."

I dried my hands and took a seat at the table. "He's been the manager for three years. The first employee left two and a half years ago. The same time Cookie's divorce happened."

Cooper jotted that under Toly's name while I ate some fries. "What else?"

"Put Cookie slash Elena on there."

He added her name. "Should I put that she owns the Gingerbread Inn?"

"Yes. And the Thrifty Maids cleaning service. Which connects her to Toly by more than blood because that's who he hired to clean the apartments."

Cooper looked up. "How many apartments are there?"

"Seven, but one's reserved for visits by management and of the six for employees, only five are currently occupied. Well, four now that Owen's gone."

"Even so, she can't be cleaning that many apartments in one day by herself. She must have help."

"Good point, but I don't know who else works for her. I was working in the shop last Wednesday, so I didn't see the crew. That's the day the cleaners come."

"Are you sure Cookie is even part of the cleaning team? How could she spare the time when she's running the B&B?"

I took a breath. "I have to tell you, I don't think the B&B is as busy as people think. I went by there, and for a place with no vacancies, there were also no people there except for the gardener. The only car in the lot was a beat-up truck with the inn's name on the side. What does Cookie drive?"

"A black Mercedes."

For a woman who'd had money troubles, she didn't seem like a woman who'd had money troubles. "That car wasn't there either."

He thought a moment. "Maybe all the guests were out when you went by."

"Maybe. But it was a rainy day. This morning, actually. And it was early enough that you'd think someone would have been there."

His gaze shifted to me. "Were you snooping?"

"Why does everyone think I snoop? I was just checking into things."

"Mm-hmm."

"Hey, somebody's got to figure this out." And technically, that was the whole reason I was here. "The sheriff wasn't interested, so that leaves me."

"Well, it's not exactly a crime to quit your job, and leaving town without notice doesn't point to foul play."

I put my elbows on the table. "No, but don't you think it's weird that they've all quit and left everything behind? And that all the notes were written on the same paper? And that none of these employees can be found? It's like they've all disappeared. Well, I think at least two of them are still living in town. They just don't look like elves anymore."

Cooper's brows were stuck in an upward position for about ten seconds. "How do you know all this?"

I stuffed a couple fries in my mouth to buy some time, then settled on the answer least likely to arouse suspicion. "I snooped. Happy?"

He laughed. "Okay, what else do you know?"

"Toly's not the easiest boss. Besides skimping on breaks and loading us up with work, he also seems to regularly turn over the responsibility for handling the shimmer on Snowy Saturdays."

"Oh, yeah, I've been in the store on one of those days. It's pretty cool. Does that take a lot of magic?"

I nodded. "Yes. And frankly if he can't handle it himself, he shouldn't be making us do it. If something were to get damaged in the store because of the snow, or if a customer was to slip on some and fall, you can bet the employee on duty would be the one who got into trouble."

As Cooper scrawled, I huffed out a breath. "Corporate wouldn't like it much either, which is probably why Snowy Saturday isn't a companywide policy."

He glanced up. "Anything else? The only picture I'm seeing right now is that Toly's a hard boss, but nothing that really points to anything besides employees quitting and not wanting to be found, which is weird, but not criminal."

I turned sideways and put my feet on the chair next to mine. "There is the whole elevator thing…"

"Nope. Not taking you down there. Already told you that."

The way he shut that topic down made me instantly decide to keep the rest of it to myself. I would have loved to get back to the Basement and look around, especially since I was sure that's the last place Owen had been, but Cooper wasn't about to help me get there. And Greyson might, but he was already working the underweb angle for me.

"Hey, I have to get back to the station." Cooper stood, putting me eye level with his utility belt. And the keycard dangling from it.

Bad thoughts started to form in my head. Good bad thoughts. I stood up and did my best to look seductive, which wasn't as easy as it sounds, considering I'd just downed about three thousand calories worth of protein and carbs. "Thanks for the lunch date."

He tucked his pen away. "You're welcome."

I sidled closer, fluttering my lashes. "You want to come back tonight and we can finish the cobbler?"

He smiled. "That would be nice. Except I won't have another evening free for four nights."

I trailed my finger down his chest. "You get a dinner break, don't you?"

His hands went to my hips. "I'm sure I can work something out."

And then, right on plan, he leaned in and kissed me.

I put my hands on his waist and kissed him back with everything that was in me. I even moaned a little, which wasn't that hard to do. I might have mentioned Cooper was a good kisser. But I laid it on heavy, pressing myself against him and running my hands over him to be as distracting as possible.

Mission accomplished, I finally broke the kiss. I tucked my hands behind my back and stepped away from him. "You'd better go now, or I might not let you."

He was heavy-lidded and drunk with pleasure. A look I remembered. And a state of being I'd been counting on. "Yeah. See you tonight."

"Tonight." I walked him to the door, keeping his gaze locked on mine until he was out in the hall. "Bye, Coop."

"Bye, Lilibeth."

I shut the door and leaned against it, my smile unstoppable. I reached into the back pocket of my jeans and pulled out the prize that kiss had earned me.

Cooper's keycard.

I waited until I was sure he was out of the building, then I went downstairs. Toly's office was dark. He was probably in the shop. Or wherever. Right now, I didn't care.

With nerves racing through me, I stood in the vestibule facing the elevator. I was about to swipe Cooper's card through the reader when my phone rang. I jumped, then caught my breath and checked the screen.

Greyson. I answered. "Hey."

"You all right? You sound funny."

"I'm fine. The ringer scared me. What's up? You find out anything about—"

"Not over the phone. I have something else I need to do, but I can be there in the next hour or so."

That was more than enough time for me to investigate and get back to my apartment. "Sounds good. And since you're now on the approved list, you can come on up."

"See you soon, princess."

"Hah-ha. Bye." I tucked my phone away and ran the card through the reader. It worked like a charm.

Thirty seconds later, I was standing in the alcove of the Basement. On my own. I grinned, unable to be anything but tickled at my own sly ingenuity. I stuck Cooper's keycard in my back pocket with my phone for safe keeping.

Then I said a little prayer he wouldn't miss it anytime soon.

I tiptoed forward to where the alcove met the main hall and looked down both directions of the corridor. No one. I took a big sniff. No trace of Owen's aftershave either, although I wondered if Greyson would have been able to pick something up. His senses were definitely keener than mine.

I turned back to look at the two locked rooms on either side of the elevator. Greyson said those rooms were above his paygrade, but Cooper was a fireman. A first responder. Surely they had access to everything.

And if they didn't, I'd do what I did best and slip under the door.

I took the keycard out again. My instincts said try the door on the right first, so I did.

As the keycard went through, the red light on the pad changed to green. Nice as ice. I turned the handle and pushed the door open. The room beyond was dark, and very little light filtered in from the dim alcove.

I didn't see a light switch so I swapped the keycard for my phone and fired up my flashlight.

The room was disappointingly empty except for a wire rack holding what looked like rolled-up vinyl banners and a wheeled cart with some folding chairs. I sighed. Greyson had been right. These rooms were storage.

I decided to check the one on the left anyway. When the light went green, I opened the door a crack and was about to stick my lit-up phone inside when a faint blue glow registered. A security light maybe. I took a step in, expecting to see more stuff that had been mothballed.

Instead, I saw where the faint blue glow emanated from. A good-sized crystal sat on top of some sort of cage-like structure. The light coming from it pulsed as if it was growing stronger. My eyes adjusted a little more and I realized there was a person inside the cage.

Owen.

I slipped inside and let the door close behind me. I blinked, trying to get my eyes to adjust further to the darkness. "Owen, can you hear me?"

No response. He was clearly unconscious and strapped into a seat in the center of an odd contraption that looked like a cross between a giant erector set and a birdcage. I stepped closer. Magic energy danced through the room. Elven magic.

The glowing blue crystal at the top was about the size of my fist. It crackled with energy and every so often, a soft moan escaped Owen.

As my eyes adjusted further, I took a closer look at him. Strands of silver wire wrapped his wrists, ankles and forehead. The strands snaked out to the cage, then wound up through the apparatus to meet at the base of the crystal.

I glanced back at Owen. The points of his ears were gone, rounded off like a humans, and he was pale. As if the life force was being drained out of him. The pieces of the puzzle I'd been trying to solve started clicking into place.

"Hang on, Owen. I'll get you out of here."

I reached for the lock on the front of the cage.

Something cracked me on the back of the head. Pain exploded through my body, and my vision filled with sparks. My hands slipped off the bars of the cage, and I fell, only catching a glimpse of a person who seemed vaguely familiar before everything went black.

I woke up with my head throbbing so hard I could barely see. I had no idea who'd hit me or how long I'd been out. I reached to brush my hair off my face and couldn't move.

I tugged at my arms. Restraints at my wrists and elbows kept me from moving anything more than my fingers. As my vision slowly returned, the bars of a cage came into focus around me. I'd been confined to the cell where Owen had been. I looked around and found him at the edge of the glow's soft circle. He was lying near the wall, facing away from me.

My heart sank at the thought that he was dead. I had to get out of here. Besides the restraints, the strands of silver were connected to me now.

"You're a busybody."

I turned my head, trying to see who'd spoken, and succeeded in making my head ache even more.

The voice was as vaguely familiar as the person I'd seen before blanking out. It took a moment for my eyes to focus and another second for my aching head to make sense of who was standing in front of me. "You?"

"Yes, me." Cookie Featherstone shook her head. "Who did you think was doing all this? My grandfather?" She laughed.

"He must be involved somehow."

"Not in a major way. All he does is help out by bringing an exceptionally gifted employee to dinner once in a while."

So that's the "date" Owen had been going on. "So when Toly checks all the employees to see how skilled they are, he's doing that for you?"

She scoffed. "Not entirely. He's also doing that so he doesn't have to concentrate so hard on running the shimmer. He'd rather spend time building his toys."

There was no point in keeping my visit to the B&B a secret now. "Then why does he have an office at your B&B?"

"He doesn't. That's my office."

"And your toy designs?"

She put her hand on one of the cage's metal bars. "Those weren't toys. Those were prototypes of more magic-gathering devices. My prototypes. I am the granddaughter of a tinker, you know."

"You're an embarrassment is what you are."

Her lip curled. "You couldn't leave it alone, could you? Nice of you to make your way down here on your own, though. Saved me the effort of getting you here." She leaned in. "And I already knew you'd been at the Gingerbread. I saw you on the security cameras. You would have been next anyway."

She straightened and glanced over at Owen. "He was just about done, so it worked out." Then she smiled. "Now I'll have extra crystals to sell this month. Bonus! And you're a strong one."

She had no idea. As my wits returned, I understood exactly what she was doing. Those puzzle pieces? All together now. And the picture was clear. Cookie was stripping the magic out of the workers with this contraption, and she was selling the crystals on the underweb. I scowled right back at her. "Stronger than you are smart."

She ignored my dig to watch a spark of blue travel up one of the silver threads and into the crystal above me. "Really strong."

Actually, she was smart enough to access the Basement. I had to know how she'd done that. "How did you get down here? Only Nocturne Falls employees have access."

She batted her lashes at me. "Date the right people, and you can lift a keycard pretty easily."

Just like I'd done. "Why do it here? Why not do this at your inn?"

Cookie stared at me, her mouth quirking up slightly. "This is a lot more private. And so convenient. And soundproof." She leaned in. "Sometimes there's screaming. And I can't have my neighbors snooping, now can I?"

Screaming? That sent a new chill through me. I had to get out of here.

She twirled my silver bracelet around her finger. "Not sure why you were hiding your light under a bushel."

Cookie obviously didn't realize I was the Winter Princess. But that's what happened to elves who left the NP and didn't bother to educate themselves on their own culture.

She continued, "You make the rest of them look practically human. Which they technically are now."

With their elven magic stripped, the workers essentially became human. She wasn't just taking their magic, she was taking their identities. No wonder Will hadn't known his name when I'd questioned him at the B&B.

Even worse, Cookie had turned him into slave labor. Like grandfather like granddaughter, apparently. I scowled at her. "You are never going to get away with this. You or your grandfather, because I don't believe for a cold second he's only bringing you employees."

She laughed. "I've been getting away siphoning

magic off the employees for years. And my grandfather has no idea what I'm doing down here."

"You expect me to believe you built this contraption?"

Anger flashed in her eyes. Good. I wanted to make her angry. "I don't care what you believe, but I built it. It's based on one of his toy ideas that went horribly wrong, but I fixed that."

"It's still horribly wrong."

"Not from my side of things. The money I make on these crystals beats what I made running that wretched B&B any day."

My hands were at my sides, but still too far away to reach my phone. And I could feel that crystal draining me. The urge to close my eyes and give in was strong. "Let me go and we can still make this right."

"You might as well save your breath." She stepped back and glanced at the crystal again. "I might get four or five out of you. Most of them give me two. Occasionally three. I should see if Grandpa Featherstone can get more like you."

While she was distracted, I pointed my fingers in her direction and called the power remaining in my veins. Ice needles shot forward. Most ricocheted off the bars, but some hit their target and buried themselves into Cookie's upper thigh.

She yelped out a curse and limped backward. She glared at me before checking her leg. It was too dark for me to tell how much damage I'd done. "That's enough of that." She pulled a fragment of blue crystal from her pocket, stuck it into the lock and turned.

The glow from the crystal above me traveled down over the cage to the floor, sealing me inside the cage with the blue light. I lifted my fingers to give her a second dose of ice, and she shook her head.

"You're just wasting your power."

I let another bolt of ice out anyway. The shards hit the blue glow and hissed into vapor. *Snowballs.* This was not looking good.

"Told you." She clucked her tongue. "The fight will go out of you by the second crystal anyway. Just relax. Being human's not so bad. I've got a room already for you at the B&B, and in a couple of months, you'll be settled into your new identity."

"Is that what you did to the other workers? Like Franny?"

"Franny's name is Leah now, and she's very happy in her new job as manager of my cleaning business. Speaking of, I could use another toilet scrubber." She grinned like that was the funniest thing ever. "You'll see. You won't remember that you ever were an elf, either."

"You're a disgrace to our people." I had to think

of something. The urge to sleep grew stronger every second.

She rolled her eyes. "This conversation is over. I'll be back in a couple of hours when you're too weak to open your pie hole."

Light burst into the room as the door opened, outlining two silhouettes in its frame. "Lilibeth?"

I'd never been so happy to hear Cooper's voice. Judging by the shape of the second silhouette, Greyson was with him. Relief washed through me. "Over here. Under the blue glow."

Cookie swung around and lifted her hands, sending shards of ice hurtling through the air like bullets. Whoa. Unexpected. Cooper threw his hands up and met the ice with a wall of heat in return. The shards disappeared in little hisses of steam.

Cookie started round two as Greyson appeared at the side of the cage. "Are you all right?"

"Yes, but I won't be for much longer."

Cookie flung a hand toward him, and shot a blast of cold at Greyson, turning him into a vampire popsicle.

I had to do something. I glanced at the crystal, then at the cage holding me, and an idea began to form. I started generating every ounce of cold I could muster.

With the cage sealed by the blue glow, the temperature inside began to drop. It wouldn't affect me, though. Outside, the ongoing battle raged between Cooper and Cookie. She'd no doubt helped herself to some of the power she'd drained off the workers, because there was no way she should be that strong.

Fortunately, Cooper's firepower was fairly impressive. He returned every one of her blasts of ice with bolts of fire.

At the first metallic whine, I glanced up. The metal struts were stressing under the intense cold. Just a little bit more now. I pushed harder, closing my eyes and dropping the temperature even lower. My head throbbed with pain. The effort of fighting the crystal's drain while producing this much cold was taking its toll. The head wound wasn't helping either. My breath puffed out of my mouth in clouds of vapor and turned into tiny snowflakes that whirled around on the freezing currents I was creating.

Almost nothing was visible beyond the foggy blue haze of the cage's confines now. One of the bars creaked like it might snap.

Cold enough.

I rocked back and forth, getting some momentum going. Finally, the chair tipped back. The silver threads snapped, and the wooden chair shattered as it landed. The cage disintegrated. I threw my arms over my face as it came down in pieces around me. Something thumped hard against my belly. I peeked through my arms. The crystal had fallen onto my stomach. I lay there for a moment, a little stunned by the impact.

Then my senses returned. I grabbed the crystal and stuck it in the pocket of my hoodie. Greyson had started to thaw, thanks to the blasts of heat Cooper was battling Cookie with.

Enough already. She needed to go down.

I built a baton of ice in my hands then whacked Cookie on the head with it. Probably the same thing she'd done to me, but I doubted she'd enjoyed it as much as I just had.

She went down hard and lay very still. I crouched down and checked the pulse in her neck. "Not dead."

Cooper walked over, staring at me like he'd seen a ghost. Which I guess technically I was. The ghost of girlfriends past. "Jayne? What the hell are you doing here?" He looked around. "Where's Lilibeth?"

Oh boy. "Long story. Lilibeth's fine. Look, I'll be happy to explain later, but first can you defrost the vampire?"

Four hours, three sheriff cars, two ambulances, and one very unhappy vampire later, the ordeal was over.

I'd gotten away with a check-up on site. My head wound had already healed, and the goose egg left behind got smaller every minute, thanks to my supernatural healing abilities.

Greyson had been carted off to the hospital to be checked over by a supernatural doc. Freezing to death couldn't really happen when you were already dead, but apparently he needed a serious infusion of blood to make him right. Once that happened, I knew Greyson would probably show up at my door.

Cookie and Toly were in holding cells at the sheriff's station. Juniper and Buttercup were at the hospital with Owen, who was never going to be fully elf again, and the shop was closed with a note on the door that said we were doing inventory.

Cooper and I, however, were back in my apartment. I was exhausted, but Cooper deserved an explanation. First, though, I owed him an apology. "I'm sorry I swiped your keycard."

"You're lucky I realized pretty quickly that you'd taken it. And that I ran into Greyson. You wouldn't be you anymore." He glared at me. "Not that you've been you since you got here."

Cooper's eyes held a storm of irritation. Which I deserved. "I didn't have a choice."

He just grunted.

I shifted the ice bag I was holding against my head. I could have frosted up my hand and used that, but the ice bag was much more dramatic and a few sympathy points from Cooper wouldn't hurt. "I'm really glad you two showed up when you did."

He sighed. "Are you going to be okay?"

I nodded. "I've already re-absorbed the magic that was drained from me." It was as simple as holding the crystal and calling the magic back into my system.

"And Owen? And the rest of the employees?"

The sigh that escaped my lips wasn't a happy one. "They've undergone physical changes that can't be undone. Might be possible to return some of their magic to them, but the crystals Cookie already sold, that magic is gone for good."

He was silent a few moments. "You were right about something bad going on."

"I just wish I'd figured it out sooner."

"You could have told me who you really were."

"I couldn't."

"Why not?"

I explained the whole thing from start to finish. And I apologized again for stealing his keycard. He still looked majorly ticked off, all arms crossed and brows knit in that judgy way of his I remembered so well.

I put the ice pack in the sink. "It's not like I came here to seduce you into my plan. Or lie to you on purpose. I didn't even know you lived in this town. That was just an unfortunate coincidence."

"I'll say," he snorted. "Too bad about Lilibeth. I was really starting to like her."

If I rolled my eyes any more today, I was risking permanent blindness. "I *am* Lilibeth. It is my middle name, you know. And you used to love me."

"Used to. Before you decided I wasn't good enough to meet your parents."

I stared at him. "I don't know what you're talking about. You're the one who told me you didn't want anything to do with me or my family." Not to mention the other things he'd said about me all those years ago.

"Because *you* didn't want anything to do with

me. I heard all about how you were so worried that I'd embarrass you in front of your parents."

I couldn't believe what I was hearing. "Back up. I never said those things. Never. I was excited to take you home and introduce you. You were the first guy who ever liked me for me, not because I was heir to the Winter Throne. And I was crazy about you." My thought process screeched to a halt. "Wait. What do you mean you *heard* about that?"

His eyes were steely. "Your buddy Lark told me all about it. That's why I broke things off with you before you could do the same to me."

I sat on the couch, feeling slightly ill. "And Lark told me you were joking in front of your friends about how you were just doing the princess so you could spend winter break at the palace." The memories came rushing back, as ugly as they had ever been. I couldn't look at him. "How you couldn't wait to see how lux your Christmas present was going to be."

He swore softly. "Jay, I never said any of that."

I risked a glance. He looked horrified. "Then why did Lark tell me all that? She was my best friend. Still is."

He barked out a harsh laugh. "Lark? Some best friend. She tried to sleep with me the day after you and I broke up."

"What? That can't be. The day after we broke

307

up, I went home for winter break and Lark…" I swallowed. The room seemed to get a little darker. The air a little harder to breathe. "Lark stayed behind. I remember now. She said she had to have a meeting with one of her professors because of a grading error."

He shook his head. "The only meeting she had was with me. I came back to my dorm that day and she was waiting for me. I made her get dressed then I kicked her out. Never saw her again after that."

"That's because a week after she came home for winter break she decided to 'find herself' in Europe. That was the last I saw of her too, for a long while. I think she's been back three times in the last ten years."

"And you're still best friends? How does that work?"

"We text." I glanced at my phone where it lay on the coffee table. "I text." I put my head in my hands. All these years the woman I'd considered my best friend had actually been my betrayer. My stomach churned with cold anger, and bitterness coated my tongue. "She broke us up. Because she wanted to get in your pants. I can't believe what an idiot I was."

The cushion sank beside me as Cooper joined me on the couch. "We were both idiots. I should have known you wouldn't have acted like that."

"And I should have known you weren't using me." I tipped my head sideways so I could see him. "You weren't, were you?"

"*No*." His breath seemed to catch in his throat. "I loved you, Jay."

My eyes stung with regret and hurt. I sat back and stared at the ceiling. "I spent the next three semesters until graduation avoiding you."

"Likewise."

We stayed like that a long time, me staring at the ceiling, Cooper staring at me. There were a thousand things unsaid, but somehow we both understood.

Finally, I straightened and sighed out a long breath. "I'm sorry."

"Me, too. Maybe we can be friends."

I nodded, my gaze focused on the coffee table. "That would be a good place to start."

"You, uh, you and Greyson...is that a thing?"

I laughed a little. "I guess. I don't know. I mean, we've gone out a few times, but we haven't exchanged promise rings or anything. What does it matter? I'll be headed back to the North Pole soon. Speaking of, I need to call my dad, tell him what happened."

Cooper nodded and stood. "I'm glad we talked. I didn't like the way I felt about how things ended."

I got to my feet, fighting a strong urge to wrap

my arms around him. "Me, too. I'd rather think of our time together fondly, you know?"

His smile was a little sad as he leaned in and tentatively kissed my forehead. "See you around, Jay."

"Yeah, you too, Coop."

He let himself out. Then I lay down on the couch and had a good cry.

I ended up falling asleep and waking up a couple hours later to banging on my door. Juniper and Buttercup were on the other side. "Hey."

They stared at me for a few long, hard seconds. Then Juniper spoke. "We get why you lied to us. It's not a hundred percent cool, but we get it."

Buttercup squinted. "And we forgive you. But you better not ever do it again."

I agreed instantly. "I won't. I swear."

Juniper crossed her arms. "Was the whole Lilibeth thing fake or was that basically you with a different name?"

"It was me with a different name. Which is really Jayne."

Buttercup rolled her eyes. "We know. And I am not calling you Your Highness."

Juniper elbowed her and mumbled, "We have to."

I laughed. "No, you don't. In fact, I'd rather you didn't."

"Good," Buttercup sniffed.

"I really don't want you to treat me any differently. Cool?"

Buttercup nodded and Juniper smiled. "Cool. So, are you okay?"

"I'm fine." I paused. "Are *we* okay?"

Buttercup smirked. "I can't believe you're the freaking Winter Princess."

I wanted to think that was a yes. "At least I'm not named after one."

She snorted and Juniper laughed. "It is pretty amazing that we had North Pole royalty right under our noses and didn't know it. We hung out and everything!" Then she frowned. "Are you sure you want to be friends with us?"

I almost teared up. "Are you kidding? I love you guys. I can't imagine anyone I'd rather be friends with."

Juniper hugged me and then Buttercup joined in, albeit a little reluctantly. I hugged them back and we stood like that until a few seconds later when Spider started crying for food.

We broke apart, laughing. I scooped Spider up and held him like a baby. "Thanks for coming to see me. I wasn't sure you'd want to."

They smiled. Juniper gave Spider a scratch on the head. "Get some rest. We'll catch up on all the good stuff tomorrow...Jayne."

I smiled. "Tomorrow."

As I closed the door, I felt as awful as I did

good. The employee situation was resolved, Cooper and I were friends again, but I was leaving soon and probably wouldn't see much of him or Greyson or Juniper or Buttercup again. Tomorrow might actually be my last day. Total suckage.

I hadn't expected that leaving would to be so tough. I fed Spider, took a shower, put on some clean clothes, and called my dad.

With Spider curled on my lap, I ran the whole thing down for him the way I had for Cooper. When I finished, pride practically wafted right through the snow globe. "Amazing, Jayne. Well done. I'm not happy you or your friends got hurt, but you did an outstanding job of working this thing out. A real chip off the old ice block."

"Thanks, Dad. I had Toly pegged wrong, though. I thought he was behind the whole thing."

"Well, he was still involved, so you were right about that. And it remains to be seen just how deeply. No, Jay, your work on this was commendable."

I smiled. It was nice to finally feel like I was good at something. "Do you have any idea who you're going to bring in as manager to replace him?"

His expression shifted, clouded with reluctance. "Your uncle Kris and I have talked it over, and we're going to close that store."

"What? You can't do that. What about Juniper and Buttercup? What about their jobs?"

"Honey, we can move them to other stores."

I couldn't stand to think of them separated. Words came out of my mouth before I really had a chance to think about them. "I want the store."

"What do you mean?"

What did I mean? "I want...to be the manager." Yelping yetis, I really did want to be the manager. "I like it here, I've made friends, and I love working in the store and with the customers. I'd be really good at running this place."

"*You* love working with customers? Human customers?"

"They're nice, Dad. Not at all like I thought."

"You have changed."

"For the better, don't you think?"

"I do."

That was a good sign. I kept at it. "Furthermore, I have more than enough power to run the shimmer, and I don't think Spider could handle the cold anyway."

My dad's eyes narrowed. "How hard did you get hit on the head?"

"Dad, I'm serious. I'm staying. You're not closing the store. This is a great location. I'll need you to send me the files of the next ten applicants on the waiting list so I can pick out some new employees. We're a little low."

"You're sure about this?"

"More than I've ever been about anything."

Smiling like a simpleton, I gave Spider's head a good scratch. I was excited about this. And not just because of Greyson. And Cooper. Juniper and Buttercup definitely figured in.

"Well, it's okay with me. I'm sure Kris won't have any issues with it either. You can take the big apartment on the third floor then. If we need to visit, we'll just stay with you."

"No. I'm staying right where I am. This place is plenty big enough. But I will expect you and Mom to visit once in a while. She owes me pie."

My dad laughed. "I'll tell her. Anything else?"

"Hmm." I thought for a moment. "We should probably discuss how much of a raise I'm getting…"

The End

Want to be up to date on all books & release dates by Kristen Painter? Sign-up for my newsletter on my website, www.kristenpainter.com. No spam, just news (sales, freebies, and releases.)

If you loved the book and want to help the series grow, tell a friend about the book and take time to leave a review!

Other Books by Kristen Painter

PARANORMAL ROMANCE

Nocturne Falls series
The Vampire's Mail Order Bride
The Werewolf Meets His Match
The Gargoyle Gets His Girl
The Professor Woos The Witch
The Witch's Halloween Hero – short story
The Werewolf's Christmas Wish – short story
The Vampire's Fake Fiancée
The Vampire's Valentine Surprise – short story

Sin City Collectors series
Queen of Hearts
Dead Man's Hand
Double or Nothing
Box Set

STAND-ALONE PARANORMAL ROMANCE

Dark Kiss of the Reaper
Heart of Fire
Recipe for Magic
Miss Bramble and the Leviathan

URBAN FANTASY

The House of Comarré series:
Forbidden Blood
Blood Rights
Flesh and Blood
Bad Blood
Out For Blood
Last Blood

Crescent City series:
House of the Rising Sun
City of Eternal Night
Garden of Dreams and Desires

Nothing is completed without an amazing team.

Many thanks to:

Cover design: Janet Holmes
Interior formatting: Author E.M.S.
Editor: Joyce Lamb
Copyedits/proofs: Angie Ramey/Marlene Engel

About the Author

Kristen Painter likes to balance her obsessions with shoes and cats by making the lives of her characters miserable and surprising her readers with interesting twists. She currently writes paranormal romance and award-winning urban fantasy. The former college English teacher can often be found all over social media where she loves to interact with readers. Visit her web site to learn more.

www.kristenpainter.com